MAGAESTRA: TESTED

KATHERINE KIM

Follow me on Instagram @katherineukim or on Facebook

Cover by Sabrina Watts at Enchanted Ink Studio

For Margaret, who threw Magaestra: Loyalties at the wall when she finished it. Best compliment ever.

Keep up with new releases, giveaways, and other antics by joining my mailing list. You'll get a free short story, news of my new releases and sales, and updates from any shenanigans I get up to!

CHAPTER 1

Faith sat at the heavy wooden table and gritted her teeth, straining. She felt a bead of sweat start to roll down her face, but couldn't spare any focus to swipe at it as she kept her attention on her task. Another push and the feather settled gently back to the tray it had come from, and she gasped in a breath.

"Not bad. Did you remember to keep pulling in fresh energy as you worked?" Detective Kenneth Lincoln asked.

Faith glared at him as she caught her breath. The dark-haired man was the first mage outside her family that she had ever met, and he was helping her to learn things she really ought to have known already.

"I did my best," she grumbled. "Moving a tiny feather like that with any accuracy using just *wind* isn't exactly the easiest thing ever, you know. That's not even a *feather* feather. It's a bit of down from your winter coat! I could do it easier and faster with my telekinesis magic."

Ken grinned and shrugged, then sent the feather through a series of loops before settling it on the table in front of Faith. "I am well aware. Just because it looks easy for me to move that with air doesn't mean that learning control wasn't difficult for me, too. I just did it fifteen years ago."

He flicked his fingers out and three candle flames flickered into existence in front of him, dancing and weaving in the air and lighting up the meeting room they sat in. "Besides, it's good for you to have more than one way to do things. It's easy for you to move things around by pushing with your magic, but by using the air to move things, you have an extra skill in your toolkit."

Faith scowled at him. The sounds of clanking weights and friendly teasing from outside the door seemed a direct contrast to the detective's smirk.

"Show off."

They sat in the basement of the Frostwalker Clan house, in a room specifically dedicated now to Faith's magic practice. She grabbed her bottle of water and twisted the cap off, and closed her eyes to focus on the cheerful sounds of some of the enforcers and sentries training in the gym that was just a few steps down a short hallway. The thought that not one of them was human made her grin, mentally.

The past few weeks had brought more changes into her life than she could even count, but these, at least, were good ones. Learning that werewolves were a real thing had sadly not been the craziest part of it all. Over the past few weeks she had been attacked, her sister kidnapped, and her *niece* kidnapped then rescued, and Faith herself had killed one vampire and saved the life of another.

They had learned about a whole world of paranormal people, creatures, and history and while Crissy was still missing, Faith and her niece Kaylee had found safety with a group of werewolves and vampires that called themselves the Frostwalker Clan. Then, there was Detective Kenneth Lincoln.

A particularly loud clang and a cheer gently rattled the door. Faith grinned but Ken grunted and glowered at the door as if he could see the people in the gym.

"How can you stay here, anyway?" he grumbled. "You can't trust them, they'll just use you for your magic and keep you locked down here or something."

Faith rolled her eyes. "They've repeatedly risked their own lives to keep me and Kaylee safe, and they've tried to rescue Crissy. They're good people, Ken."

"You can't trust 'em," he grumbled, but this was far from the first time he had tried to convince her to leave the Clan house. Ken didn't trust non-human paranormals, and Faith could admit that she understood why.

World War Two had been the human extension of a paranormal war waged by a particular coven of vampires and their allies, specifically against human mages. That war had caused mages to be hunted nearly to extinction and so many families were destroyed that it hurt Faith's heart to think about it.

She had once visited the Holocaust Museum during a trip to Washington DC and she had left badly shaken at what humans could do to each other. Now she knew that was only half the story. The vampires had hunted mages specifically to drink the magic in their blood, then used the abilities they gained from that magic to try to assert their *vampiric superiority* over the rest of the world. Ken's family had been just as directly affected as her own, the only difference being that Ken's family had known the history and hers hadn't.

Then, of course, his parents hadn't been killed in a car accident, so he had been able to finish his training as a mage rather than get shipped off to LA to get raised by an aunt who thought things like magic were only in the movies the town was known for.

"I can trust the Frostwalkers, Ken. You know I can, too." Faith was not going to hear a word against her new friends, and Ken knew it. Well, he did now. She had gotten sick of his constant sniping and lit into him at one point, and since then this was about as bad as it got.

"Well, you ready to go again?" he asked. He nodded at the damn feather. "Practice makes perfect. And make sure you're drawing new energy from the environment. It's not as easy inside a building like this, but it's plenty possible."

Faith glared at his smirk and then took a deep breath and started the feather moving again, swooping and dipping to sketch through a whole set of geometric shapes in the air.

A few hours later and the sweat was making her hair cling to her neck and around her face. She was as tired and sore as if she had been in one of Tamika's self-defense training sessions rather than seated at a conference table the whole time.

"Do it again," Ken said.

"Not a chance," Faith answered, slumping back in her chair. "I'm all tapped out for the moment."

Ken grinned, and it startled her. He wasn't really a grinning kind of guy. Well, at least not anywhere near the Frostwalker Clan, even though he agreed that this room in the basement of the clan house was probably the safest place for Faith to practice.

"It's like exercise. Gotta push a bit to build your magic muscles."

"Yeah, well, my magic muscles are jelly at this point," Faith grumbled. She was about to say something more when there was a hesitant knock on the door.

Faith and Ken frowned at each other. They were

supposed to be undisturbed while they were in here, except in an emergency, since losing concentration while juggling fireballs wasn't healthy for anyone.

"Yes?" Ken called.

There was a long moment of silence before a very soft answer came. "Aunt Faith?"

Faith and Ken exchanged a glance and he got up to open the door. On the other side was Kaylee, hunched in a bit but with her chin up, like she was going to be brave despite everything.

"Aunt Faith, can I come in?"

"Sure, Kaylee-bee, what can I do for you?" Faith opened her arms as the child climbed into her lap and snuggled in. Faith exchanged a glance with Ken, who looked equally worried.

"What's up? Where's Jake? I hardly ever see you two apart anymore." Faith wanted to know what was going on with her niece. It could be anything at this point. Over the past few weeks, the child had dealt with rogue werewolf attacks, her mother being kidnapped, then getting kidnapped herself. She had her newly rescued mother snatched away from them mid-rescue, faced down monstrous dog creatures and vampires, dodged more attacks, and then saw her new best friend suddenly turn into a wolf pup and her favorite teacher in a hospital bed.

All in all, it was maybe more surprising that Kaylee was as cheerful as she was usually.

"Jake is practicing not shifting by accident. Mr. Greg and Marc are helping him." Kaylee answered.

"Ah." Faith nodded. It made sense. werewolves didn't usually shift until much closer to puberty. Jake wasn't even in kindergarten yet but had shifted during an attack on the Frostwalker Clan house in a bid to protect Kaylee. Now, though, he had to learn control so he didn't accidentally shift in front of normal humans.

"Am I going to turn into a wolf, too?" Kaylee's eyes turned up to stare at Faith.

"Well, we talked about this a bit before, remember?" Faith sighed. She was so out of her depth here. God, how did Crissy manage? "Your mom is a mage, so maybe you'll have magic you can use to do spells instead."

Kaylee sighed and snuggled in closer. "Where is Mommy? I miss her and want her to come home now."

The sadness in the girl's voice grabbed Faith's heart and squeezed. She tried to answer but the words stuck in her throat.

"There are a lot of people out looking for your mom right now," Ken spoke up. He scooted his chair around the table and leaned close to Kaylee so she could see him without moving too much.

"There's the human police out doing everything they can. Your mom and I are looking. Your friends here are looking, too, and probably breaking as many laws as they can while doing so." Ken's expression darkened for a moment before he shook himself and smiled gently at the little girl. "We haven't found her yet, but we will. And she'll be here before you cast your first spell or turn furry the first time. Okay?"

Kaylee sniffled and nodded.

"The important thing is to stay safe so that we're here when we do find your mom. Right? So we're staying inside the house unless we have some of our friends with us," Faith added.

"I know. A whole bunch of us went down to the creek this morning. Miss Tamika is really good at catching frogs. Did you know that?" Kaylee looked up at Faith, the worry in her eyes starting to recede a bit.

"I did not know that, but Miss Tamika is good at a lot of things, so I'm not surprised," Faith answered.

"I bet Miss Tamika is pretty good at catching all sorts of things," Ken added. His voice was light and cheerful, but when Faith glanced over Kaylee's head his eyes held a lack of trust in the wolves.

The three of them kept talking for a while, reassuring Kaylee that she was safe and that everything was being done to find Crissy, and that it didn't matter if she was a werewolf or a mage, she was still important and loved. After half an hour or so, a slightly panicked voice called from down the hallway "Kaylee?"

"She's in here, Tamika!" Faith called back.

The door burst open and Tamika's eyes went right to Kaylee, still sitting in Faith's lap. "Sweet lord, Sugar, don't scare me like that! We didn't know where you were! Half the enforcers are out in the woods looking for you!" Tamika pulled her phone out and tapped at it, apparently sending a text to the rest of the team that the girl was found, safe, and still in the house.

"Kaylee," Faith used her Serious Grownup Voice. "Did you sneak away to come down here?"

"Well. I was upstairs in the den watching TV and coloring while Jake had his practice and then the show ended and I was bored and then another show started but it was dumb and then the mom in it went on a trip and I started thinking about my mommy and then I came to find you." Kaylee delivered the whole explanation without even pausing for breath. "I didn't mean to be sneaky."

"I see," Faith nodded.

Tamika sighed through a grin, "Sweetie, I need to know where you are or--"

"Kaylee!"

Tamika stepped aside as Aldric came rushing into the

room and scooped the girl up into his arms. Kaylee giggled and wrapped herself around the tall, dark man. Faith took a moment to appreciate the sight of the dangerous vampire's clear relief at finding the preschooler. His strong arms were wrapped around the child, supporting her carefully and he had his head bent over her so that all Faith could see well was his dark brown hair and the back of Kaylee's head, one lopsided pigtail sticking out.

"I'm okay Uncle Aldric, I just needed to see Aunt Faith," Kaylee said, her voice muffled by his shoulder. "I didn't mean to scare everyone."

Faith saw shock sweep through his eyes at the title, then joy spread over his face. "I'm just glad you are safe. That's the most important thing to me. That you and your aunt are safe."

"Okay. I'm sorry," Kaylee leaned back and smiled at him. "Is Jake done with his dad yet?"

"I think they may be finished soon, yes. Perhaps Tamika can take you to find him?" Aldric nodded.

"Let's go, Sugar. It's my turn to read you the riot act over disappearing like that. Then we'll get some ice cream and find Jake. Sound good?" Tamika held her hand out to the girl as Aldric set her back on her feet. The pair headed back out the door and down the hallway, the beads in Tamika's braids clacking softly when she shook her head.

"Well, I think that was more excitement than I needed when I'm this worn out," Faith sighed, slumping back in her chair. "I don't think I can keep working, Ken."

"Yeah," he grumbled. "Seems like we're done for today. If you get some time later, keep practicing."

Faith snorted.

"Would you like some coffee, or a snack?" Aldric asked. He was trying to be polite to Ken, and Faith appreciated it, in the face of Ken's prickliness. Okay, in the face of his occasionally overt hostility.

The man did not like paranormals.

"I'm fine. I'll just head out." Ken stood up and stretched. "Call me later, Faith. We'll chat." And with that he headed out the door, his footsteps fading.

Faith sighed. "I could use a cup of coffee," she said, reaching her hand out to Aldric, who took it and tugged her gently to her feet. "And a snack. And a nap."

A smile curved across his face. "I can arrange all those things."

CHAPTER 2

"I wish I knew what to say to Kaylee. I'm much better at being the fun, silly aunt than this serious kid-raising stuff." Faith pressed her back closer into Aldric's side and he ran his hand up and down her arm.

"I am simply relieved that she did not wander off as we were afraid of," Aldric said. "When Tamika looked over and she wasn't in the den, we were all afraid for the worst."

Faith nodded. "I think she gets that now. She's a pretty smart kid."

"That she is, and you are doing an excellent job, considering the circumstances," Aldric said.

"I called her preschool this morning. They were very understanding about everything when I said that she probably isn't coming back this next year." Faith sipped her coffee and the bitter scent was soothing, layered on top of Faith's own. "They were also glad to hear that Greg Honeyford was recovering when I told them we had taken him in. I told them that we were at the police station talking about Crissy when we heard he'd been rescued and offered to take him in. I think he's going to be fired, though."

"I believe Marc has offered him a position teaching here. Jake cannot attend a public school until he learns to control his shifts very well. And Greg cannot exactly go out in public already healed from that ordeal. The police have photographs of his injuries, after all, and they are not the sort that humans recover from quickly."

Faith nodded and sighed and sipped her coffee as they let the conversation die. The sofa in his office was comfortable, and Aldric was glad Marc had insisted he have it. It gave him the perfect place to sit, snuggled up to Faith while she sipped her coffee and relaxed for a few moments. Faith's back curved into his side and she cuddled happily under his arm, pulling it around her waist while she tucked her feet under a blanket.

Aldric had a file of information on the Goldfang Stalker members they were holding that he was re-reading in the hopes that he would find a clue as to who the vampires working with that pack were. He had asked Frankie to help him, since the man was still grieving and needed to feel proactive in going after the people who killed his fiancée during their first attempt at rescuing Crissy.

The man had taken Mia's death very hard, and Aldric wished that there was more they could do, but grief had its own timeline, after all.

"What are you thinking about?" She asked.

"Frankie."

Faith sighed. "It sucked what happened to Mia. I feel so guilty about it. I mean, I know it wasn't my fault, but…"

Aldric nodded.

"I can understand why he's standoffish with me. I don't blame him at all. He's nice to Kaylee, though," she added.

"Is he rude to you?" Aldric asked. He hadn't noticed much change in Frankie's attitude, aside from the air of sadness that clung to him now. "I can talk to him."

"Nah. I don't have to be best friends with everyone. I'm worried about him, though. He's in so much pain." She scrunched up her face and shrugged. "I know how he feels, a bit. It will take some time but he'll recover."

Aldric nodded again. She wasn't wrong. He would heal, and it would take time. Hopefully someday he could regain the outgoing friendliness that had drawn Mia to him in the first place.

Right now, however, Faith seemed content with this, curling into his side while they talked. It was a new development, and one he enjoyed a great deal. It started after they had been trapped in a cave the week previous and Faith had forced him to drink some of her blood to prevent his death. Even a vampire can be killed, after all. But since that day, once she had forced him to stop avoiding her, they had grown much closer.

"So I finished that book. The one about the vampire rescuing the werewolf princess? It was completely bonkers." Faith shook her head and laughed softly. "I *know* that shifters don't howl at the moon like that, but it was a neat trick to help him find her after she got kidnapped by the evil king."

Aldric nodded. "I told Marc he should read that one and he came back and threw it at my head when he finished it."

"I did like them together though," she sighed. "It's such a ridiculous trope, vampires and werewolves locked in mortal enmity forever, but it worked as something for them to overcome."

Aldric chuckled. "There was a time during the war that

factions split off, it is true, but it has never quite reached that level of enmity across whole species."

Faith sighed and snuggled closer into his side. "These books are really silly, but I'm glad that they're so inaccurate on that subject. It's a nice thought, though. That there's someone out there, a soulmate for you."

Aldric huffed a quiet laugh into her hair before kissing her head softly. "There is no mystical force, no fate or goddess pairing souls together, no. But there is a... a tradition perhaps I could call it? The idea of a soulmate is not unknown to us, after all. And yes, wolves do call them mates. I like the idea of a beloved, like in many of the books about my kind. The main difference between fiction and real life is that we choose them, rather than allowing some mystical universal force to select them for us."

Faith wiggled around to peer up at him. "What do you mean?"

"Do you recall when I told you about my parents? About how my mother died soon after my father did because they were bonded?"

She nodded.

"They knew that they were perfect for each other and that they would not wish to live apart, so they performed a ritual that bound their lives together. They joined their lives so closely that when my father was killed, my mother followed him within days. She was sad to leave me, but we all knew that she would have likely pined away even without the bond. She died, surrounded by family, and excited to see my father again."

Aldric smiled and knew it was not a fully happy expression. He loved his parents and missed them terribly, but he also remembered how they had lived for each other. It had been a romance novel sort of love, and he knew that was one reason he had never dated too seriously. He had hoped to find something like they had, and he always felt some-thing lacking with the few serious relationships he had attempted.

"Wow," Faith said on a sigh. "That's both the sweetest thing I've ever heard and heartbreakingly tragic."

Aldric nodded because there was no other answer. Faith was right.

"But Uncle Eldridge didn't bond with your aunt?"

"No." he shook his head, then rested his cheek on her hair. "My aunt was a wonderful woman, and loved us all very much, but they decided not to take that step. It's very personal and needs to be carefully considered. Uncle Eldridge knew that if my aunt died he would want to stay living with his chil-dren, and she felt the same way. They still loved each other very much, though. It was simply more of a human historical romance story rather than a contemporary paranormal one."

Faith chuckled and Aldric smiled at the sound, and at the memories of the love he had grown up watching.

"And werewolves do the same thing?" she asked after a few minutes.

"They have something similar, yes. I do not know about mages," Aldric frowned in thought. "The way it works for us, you see, is that we are creatures of magic, and our bonds share that. We can share it with human partners as well, which will have many of the effects written about in the books. I sometimes wonder if some of those books aren't written by vampires or werewolves themselves."

Faith laughed again and shifted around to swing her legs over his and leaned forward to rest her head back on his shoulder. She handed him her empty coffee cup to put on the side table and draped her arm over his chest, and something inside his soul settled.

"I wonder if mages do have something like that. I'll

have to ask Ken if he knows," she said. "Have you ever thought about doing that? Binding your life to someone else?"

"I had not, until recently. Not since I was a child and dreaming of my future," Aldric said, slowly. He knew that it was far too soon to discuss that sort of thing with Faith. They had only just met, really. Just a month earlier and neither had ever heard of the other. But they had been together through a great deal of pressure. Situations where a person's true self is often revealed, and he had learned that Faith was loyal, fierce, protective... She cared deeply for those she chose to surround herself with, and she fought for them with everything she had.

Aldric risked a glance down at her and found her biting her bottom lip to hold back a smile as she stared at where her fingers idly stroked his chest.

After a moment the smile faded. "Do you think I'm a bad sister?"

Aldric blinked at the abrupt change of topic.

"What? Why do you ask that?"

"Because I'm sitting here with you talking about romance novels and true love in real life and Crissy is still out there, somewhere. She's been gone for weeks now, and I'm curled up on your lap, flirting." Faith sighed.

"You have protected your niece, found allies, and attempted two rescues thus far," Aldric said. "You are not sitting idly, enjoying life while your sister suffers. But you cannot take on a burden of guilt for taking what joy you can when you can. Should the worst happen and we never find your sister, would you prefer to live your life miserable in penance?"

Faith sighed. "No, I know. But..." She grimaced and shook her head, her cheek rubbing against his shoulder.

Aldric wrapped his arms around her and tried to surround her with himself.

"You have friends working with you to find her. We are doing everything we can to learn who took her from the lodge and where they are keeping her. It is unlikely that they took her for the usual, human reasons so that at least should reassure you some."

"But what if she's scared? Or being starved? Or..." Her shudder broke Aldric's heart. He thought it likely that she was being harmed. He thought it was extremely likely that she was being involuntarily fed from by greedy vampires who felt that humans were nothing but prey and that human mages were there to provide vampires with extra powers.

"If she has been abused, then when we find her we will help her heal," he said. "Just like we did for Greg Honey-ford. Marc has claimed her as a Frostwalker Clan member. She is family to us as well, now, as are you and Kaylee. We will find her and we will help her."

Faith bit her lip and frowned for a long moment before she nodded. "Thank you, Aldric."

Aldric wrapped his arms around her and bent down to kiss her hair. "Anything you need, love," he whispered so quietly he wasn't certain she heard. "I'm here."

CHAPTER 3

The rest of the day was almost dull in comparison to playing with her magic or settling the nerves of a stressed child. Cuddling with Aldric was the best part, though. Faith always felt more confident after he held her, even if it was just for a moment. Like his presence helped her find her footing again, even if he did or said nothing.

She wondered what it was like to be magically bound to someone like that. The way Aldric talked about it...

Faith knew that real life wasn't like the romance novels she had taken to reading since she got here, but boy did it sound nice. To know that there was someone always there for you, dedicated and loving and protective. And she wasn't going to lie to herself: she liked feeling that around Aldric. She snuggled deeper into his arms and nuzzled against his shoulder, just so she could feel him stroke his hand up and down her back like she knew he would.

Was it possible to fall flat on your face in love in three weeks?

Was it fair to Crissy that Faith did exactly that while her sister was god knew where suffering god knew what?

That question was one of many that were gnawing at her in the cover of night when she couldn't sleep. She was about to bring it up again, whether she had any right to feel content while Crissy was missing when the doorbell rang. Faith sat up and looked toward the hallway, then back to Aldric, and she could tell he was listening as one of the enforcers opened the door. One of them was always near each of the doors since the raid on the lodge where they almost rescued Crissy.

Aldric stiffened and frowned. "Come. We must deal with this." He stood and turned to help her up. She put her hand in his and let him tug her to her feet before they headed to the front of the building.

The Frostwalker Clan House was huge and to the unaware looked more like an exclusive hotel or resort. Aldric's office was beside Marc's own, just around the corner from the entry hall. Once they had stepped out the door, Faith could hear voices. Tamika's and...

"Aunt Lucy?"

Faith dropped Aldric's hand and dashed around the corner to see that she wasn't hearing things.

"There you are, sweetie! You really are alive and not dead in a ditch somewhere, not that I would have known that, mind you. You've missed our weekly call twice now, and you didn't sound right on the one before that," Aunt Lucy said. Her hair was streaked with grey now, instead of the mahogany brown Faith still expected to see, but it was pulled back in her usual ponytail and her earrings fairly danced with her worry and irritation.

"Now then, show me my other girls and we can sit down for some explanations." Aunt Lucy stepped inside, brushing right past Tamika, who blinked in surprise. "Be a dear and pull my bags inside, please? I'm not as young as I once was and the cab driver has gone already."

"Um..."

"It's all right, Tamika," Aldric said from just behind Faith, which was a good thing since Faith was still gaping at the sight of her aunt, who should be in LA, not way up here near the Oregon border. And definitely not in the front hallway of the Frostwalker Clan of paranormals who were in the middle of a damned pack war and hunting down possibly rogue vampires to boot.

"Aunt Lucy!"

Kaylee barreled into the hallway, not stopping until she leaped into Lucy's arms.

"Oh my gosh, what are you doing here? You have to see the playset in the backyard, it's the most amazing playset ever and Jake and I put Tamika in jail there all the time and she pushes us on the swings *so high* and it's the most fun ever and when we can't play outside Jake's dad has *so many movies!* They have all the movies and their tv is ginormous! It's so cool!"

Kaylee paused to take a breath and Lucy jumped into the slight pause.

"That sounds wonderful, Kaylee-bee! I'm so excited to hear all about your new friends! But whatever are you doing here?" Lucy transferred her gaze to drill into Faith. "I went to the cabin, and some strange man told me to come here. He gave directions to the cab driver and then closed the door in my face."

"That was Rod. When he's sleepy he loses his manners," Tamika rolled her eyes. "I bet he called Marc to let us know you were coming, but lord knows if that man has his phone on him. He probably called you, too, Aldric. What's your excuse?"

She smirked at him and put Lucy's suitcase and small carry-on style bag on a bench at the side of the door. Aldric ignored her, but patted his pocket and frowned.

"Indeed. Would you go let Marc know we have a guest?" Aldric asked. "I will show Miss Lucy into the den and arrange for refreshments."

"You got it, sugar." Tamika winked and turned to head outside to the wooded area that most of the clan used to shift in some privacy, then called back over her shoulder. "And find out what happened to Kenya? She's supposed to be on Kaylee duty now."

Faith felt Aldric's hand press into her back, warm and strong.

"Come right this way, ma'am. It will be much more comfortable in the den than standing around in the entry." Aldric gestured to the left, and Kaylee hopped down and tugged on Lucy's hand, but the woman herself was peering at Faith who hadn't managed to speak since her first astonished outburst.

"Well, sweetie? Is that a good plan?" Lucy asked.

Faith shook herself out of her stupor. "Uh, yeah. Yes. The den's got a wonderful view of the backyard. You can see the play area, even. Kaylee's eyes almost leaped out of her head the first time she saw it." She tried to keep her tone steady and her face free of any sort of tells. Aunt Lucy had always known when she or Crissy were hiding something. And the secrets Faith had now were way bigger than a plan to sneak out to a party at a boy's house in high school.

Kaylee tugged Lucy's hand to drag her over to the window in the den and after asking if she would prefer coffee or tea, Aldric bowed and left them to head to the kitchen.

"Wow, Kaylee-bee. That is a serious play structure." Lucy whistled low and nodded. "I can see why you're so eager to show me. That thing could accommodate a whole class of kids!"

"It's so cool when all the kids come over and then everyone can play, but Jake is the only one that lives here. Well, me too, I guess, but it was so fun when everyone came over! We played the best game of tag and then there was so much food and we all snuck cake into the clubhouse and Deanna's big sister said we shouldn't have food in the clubhouse 'cause we'd attract pests, and then--" Kaylee's eyes got huge and she looked wildly at Faith for a moment. "And then they went home and that's all. Come look at the movies!"

Kaylee scampered to the wall with the entertainment system. "Jake's dad buys most of them so they stay on the internet, but he's got a bunch here, too. He says that it's better to have a physical backup just in case, so he gets discs with Jakes favorites and he went and bought some of mine that he didn't have and they came in the mail and we had a movie party and we watched Jake's favorite movie which is The Incredibles which is so good and then we watched Moana cause that's my favorite, then we watched something Jakes Dad likes called Howl's Moving Castle and it was a little bit scary but not too much and the end was really nice and then we had pancakes for dinner!"

Lucy's eyes were wide and sparkling with laughter by the time Kaylee slowed down to take a breath. Even Faith had relaxed, and when he brought a cart with coffee and snacks on it, Aldric grinned as the words flowed over the room.

"Did you know that Howl's Moving Castle is a book, as well? It's a bit different than the movie, but I think it is quite good. Perhaps we could find it and read it together?" Aldric said.

"Really?" Kaylee bounced up and launched at Aldric, who caught her easily. "Promise?"

"I am a man of my word, Miss Kaylee. I shall look for my copy later this evening."

"You're the best, Uncle Aldric!" Kaylee said, squeezing him before jumping around and racing out the door. "Jake! *Jake!* Uncle Aldric has the *book!*"

All three adults stared at the empty doorway and listened to the fading thumps of Kaylee's footsteps. After a moment of silence, Lucy's bright laughter broke in.

"Well, she seems to be just fine. That's quite a relief to an old woman." The laughter in her voice was clear as daylight, and Faith felt herself relaxing just a bit.

"Aunt Lucy, what are you doing here?" Faith finally felt like she had her brain unscrambled enough to catch up with the moment.

"Well, like I said. You've dodged several of our weekly calls, and when I called you, worried, you either didn't answer or brushed me off as quickly as you could. I may not be your mother, but I did raise you. You and Crissy are my girls and when you both drop off the planet and start avoiding me, I know damned well something isn't right. And don't think I haven't noticed that you haven't called Crissy down to see me." Lucy fixed her with a sharp look, then glanced over to Aldric and swept an assessing gaze over him. "Now, introduce me properly to your friend here, and tell me what the hell is going on."

Aldric smiled and bowed to Lucy as he handed her a cup of coffee and a small plate with some cookies on it. "My name is Aldric Donnelly, ma'am. It is a great pleasure to meet you. Faith has told me some about her childhood, and I am very glad that she and her sister had you to rely on."

"I am glad to meet you as well, though my niece has told me nothing whatsoever about you," Lucy raised a brow at him. "Though anyone who so cheerfully promises to read to children as a method of distracting them seems a solid enough person to start this conversation with. Am I to meet this mysterious Jake as well? And his parents? And where is Crissy? You won't distract me so easily."

"You will get to meet me right now, Miss Latham," Marc said. He strode into the room and extended his hand to shake. "I'm Marc Keller, and it's a pleasure to meet you. I guess you could say this is my house, but it feels more like a circus tent most days. Welcome."

A shriek from outside the window drew everyone's attention as two small blurs dashed to the playset. Tamika, Ori, and Kenya following behind a bit slower.

"Well, at least I know Kaylee's happy and healthy. And not one of you has answered my question yet." Her expression could make hardened warriors shiver, and Faith winced, knowing that she didn't want to have to tell this woman about... well... anything.

Faith fumbled though trying to form a complete sentence. "Um, Crissy.... That is we—"

"Crissy has been kidnapped, Miss Latham," Marc jumped in. "We had hoped to have her back, safe and sound before worrying you."

Lucy's gaze frosted over and she turned to Faith. She didn't say anything, just raised an eyebrow at her and waited for details.

"Is that so?" She said after a few moments of silence. The demand for information was more than clear in her tone, and Faith could easily hear the fear her aunt was holding back. Panic and hysteria were not things Aunt Lucy was prone to, thank goodness.

"Um, she, uh." Faith swallowed. This woman raised them, she wasn't going to attack Faith because of events outside her control. She might be mad that Faith didn't call her right away, but, she wouldn't be mad for long.

"We were attacked. Kaylee and I, I mean. At the cabin. That's why Rod is staying there right now and we're here," she started. Marc nodded when she glanced over at him and she felt Aldric's hand on her back, his thumb stroking gently up and down her spine. "The guy who was Crissy's one-night stand somehow found out that she had Kaylee and came to kidnap them both, but when I fended off his, um, his thugs long enough for Aldric to show up to beat them and get me and Kaylee away, he went after Crissy. We haven't been able to find her yet, but everyone who's investigating thinks that she's not too far away. It's too personal a situation, and they still want Kaylee for some reason."

Faith was very pleased with herself for not letting any paranormal information slip.

"Everyone who is investigating?" Aunt Lucy asked, her eyes narrowing. "You mean the police, I should hope."

"Yes. Detective Lincoln has been here a lot, and I know he's working hard to track down the people involved. And Aldric's cousin is doing some unofficial investigating, too, since he's a computer whiz." Faith scrunched up her face and shrugged "He's not hampered by all the red tape and official nonsense that the police are he says, and Ken-- Detective Lincoln-- has very carefully not asked too much about it. I don't think he wants to know where any anonymous tips come from in case Leo finds anything."

Aunt Lucy hummed and sipped her coffee, letting the information turn over in her mind. She eyed the way Aldric stayed close to Faith and glanced at Marc, who sat quietly drinking from his cup, then outside where Kaylee was dragging Tamika into the playset prison again, and Kenya and Ori were clearly on guard duty without being too stiff about it. Faith held her breath when a sentry stepped out of the shadows of the tree line for a moment before fading back into the brush. If Aunt Lucy saw them, she didn't say anything.

Hopefully, she just thought it was a dog at this distance.

She turned back to raise an eyebrow at Faith and set her coffee cup down carefully on the side table by her elbow.

"That seems like a fair number of people for watching those kids out there," Lucy said, slowly. "And I have heard the movement in the rest of the house, so I know there are more people here than just us and them." She nodded outside. "Not to mention that Rod fellow back at the cabin."

"When I offered Faith and Kaylee a safe place to stay, my people and I took that promise seriously," Marc nodded. "They don't look it, but those three out there are some of the fiercest fighters I know, and they adore Kaylee and Jake both. They couldn't be in better hands."

"And I give you my word as the head of security here that every precaution is being taken to make sure that Faith and Kaylee are both safe here while we search for Crissy," Aldric added with a slight bow.

"You say that this hoodlum was the man that fathered Kaylee? Why would he try to kidnap her instead of sending a lawyer? It doesn't make sense." Lucy pursed her lips and narrowed her eyes at Faith.

"Faith?" she asked. "You trust these men? And those folk out there?"

"I do," Faith said, with a nod. "Completely. These are good people. They didn't have to step in to help us, but they did, and they even fought off another attempt at snatching us. Ori got hurt and just finished healing up, and he's still out there on watch."

Lucy nodded again. "That's good enough for me then." Her words were brisk and final like a decision had been made and she was moving to the next problem. "Do you suppose it has something to do with the gifts your mother passed down to you girls, and I assume to Kaylee as well? It's not like this lowlife could just tell a judge about wanting to control some mages, after all."

"Wh-- what?" Faith's hand shook so hard that Aldric took her coffee cup and sat it on the table before taking her hand in his. She knew that she was gaping like a fish in a boat, but couldn't seem to stop.

Aunt Lucy just huffed and rolled her eyes. "You girls always thought you could pull the wool over my eyes like I didn't already know everything. You two have never been as careful or clever as you thought you were. So, I'm asking again." Lucy leaned forward and flicked her eyes over Aldric's now blank countenance. "Was Crissy taken because of you girls' magic or not?"

CHAPTER 4

Faith sputtered and trembled and all Aldric could do was put his arm around her in support. Marc had gone very still, watching Lucy. Aldric studied the woman again, from her faux careless hairstyle to her sensible but stylish shoes, and every inch of the woman said *competent, intelligent, and determined.* She might look at first glance like an amiable older woman, but Aldric had enough experience in his life to be wary.

"What are you talking about, Aunt Lucy?" Faith asked. Her voice was too high-pitched and uneven to be taken as it was intended, even if Lucy had been a less astute sort of woman.

Lucy sighed and deflated slightly. "Oh, Faith. I've known about your mother's family since the day your parents found out they were going to *be* parents." Lucy sat back and swept her fingers over her forehead. She gave Aldric another assessing stare then turned it on Marc, who returned it steadily.

The corner of Lucy's mouth twitched upward and a

gleam appeared in her eye while Faith just sat there, stunned. Lucy nodded.

"You seem to have found some very determined protectors. Good." She raised her brow at Marc. "I don't know what your story is, but I think I can guess. I will tell you this once, though. It doesn't matter in the slightest what you are, if you hurt my girls I will come for you and I am more dangerous than I look."

It was Marc's turn to fend off a smile. "I give you my word, as I gave it to Faith and Kaylee themselves. They will be protected with everything we can call upon. As for your threat," Marc did grin now. "You will have to get in line, I suspect."

She turned back to Aldric, who kept his face as blank as he could.

Lucy smirked at him regardless. "I had noticed, yes."

"Aunt Lucy!" Faith slumped and hid her face in her hands. After a moment she sat up again. "What do you mean you knew about Mom's family? What did you know? And what do you mean we weren't as clever as we thought we were? You'd better start explaining."

Lucy's gaze softened. "When your mom found out she was pregnant with Crissy, she and your dad knew that they needed to find someone to name as guardian, in case the worst happened. So they came to me." She paused and sipped her coffee and stared into the cup, lost in her memories for a moment. "They told me about the magic, and about what had happened to her family, and about how much danger there was for a mage in the world. I didn't believe them, of course. It sounded so outlandish! Magic and evil vampires and hunters and government conspiracies... It's the stuff of the movies I was working on, not real life."

"You know about vampires?" Aldric asked. "What else?"

Lucy grinned now, the gleam back in her eye. "I know about vampires and werewolves and all sorts of things. So don't think you're fooling me, young man. I saw that wolf in the trees a few minutes ago. I know what you all are."

And now it was Aldric's turn to be amused. "I doubt that, somehow. And I am older than I appear," he said. "*Young lady.*"

That made her eyebrows shoot up and a look of apprehension washed over her. Her whole body tensed.

"Aunt Lucy, Aldric is not an enemy," Faith jumped in. "He damn near died trying to save Crissy from those assholes, and I won't have you thinking whatever it is that you're thinking right now. I know that look. That's the look you get right before you take someone down."

"Take someone down?" Marc asked.

Faith snorted. "Don't let the innocent, helpless woman act fool you. Aunt Lucy does Krav Maga for fun in her spare time."

Lucy huffed and settled herself. "I have also taken up knitting," she said primly.

Faith rolled her eyes. "My point is that whatever it is you're thinking, you are not allowed to attack Aldric, do you understand me?"

Lucy eyed her niece for a long moment. Then she turned her eyes back to Aldric, assessing him all over again, this time for danger rather than trustworthiness. Aldric simply sat and let her judge him. He could understand being cautious if she was told anything about how much terror a handful of his kind caused around the world.

"I suppose I wouldn't judge all humans on the actions

of a few murderers. I shouldn't judge you by the actions of a few psychopaths either," she said at last.

"Thank you." Aldric bowed his head. "I have sworn to protect Faith and Kaylee with my life, and I will not go back on my word."

"I feel like we've gotten off track slightly," Marc said. "Since we're all friends here, and we all know about the paranormal world, let's start over. I am Marc Keller, leader of the Frostwalker Clan, and werewolf. This is Aldric Donnelly, my second in command and Head Enforcer for the clan, and one of our vampire members. Faith and Kaylee have both accepted membership in our clan as well, and while we have not been able to discuss it with her in person, I have claimed Crissy as ours as well to underpin our rescue efforts. She is family and that is enough."

He leaned forward. "We do not abandon our own."

"Excellent." Lucy nodded. "You say you have tried to rescue my niece already?"

Faith grimaced and started to tell Lucy the whole story, from what Crissy had told her of the creepy man in town hanging about near Kaylee's preschool, through the attack at the cabin and Crissy's kidnapping. Aldric took over for a moment when she stumbled over the near rescue of Crissy at the lodge and how the surprise attack of the strange vampires had caused them to lose Crissy again. Then he faltered when he tried to tell the story of the raid on the camp in the nearby forest.

"Aldric was dying, stuck under that damn boulder. I couldn't move it, even with my magic and he was too weak to help," Faith's voice broke. "I wasn't going to let him die." She glared at Lucy, full of defiance, daring her aunt to speak out against her actions.

Lucy's eyebrow rose and a small smile graced her face. "I see."

"He tried to refuse!" Faith grumbled. "Can you believe that? There I am bleeding thanks to the damn fall anyway, sitting in the dark, scared to death that he was about to die himself, and he wouldn't freaking feed! He *argued* with me about it!"

Marc was grinning now and Lucy's smile had widened as Faith got more vehement. "It sounds like he should know by now how stubborn you are."

Faith just growled quietly. Lucy just laughed.

"Well," she said after a moment. "I suppose you're all right after all. I'm sure you understand my concerns. Their mother didn't have a whole story to work from, just the warnings from her own parents to stay away from vampires at all costs. Werewolves were slightly less of a concern, but to be avoided if possible anyway."

Aldric nodded. He understood, and as general advice went it made sense for Magaestra to be warned away from other paranormals, considering what had happened. Vampires, being long-lived, also had long memories. Not all the vampires that survived the war were fighting on the side of freedom and life.

"Yes, ma'am. But one of the core tenants of the Frost-walker Clan is respect for others. Whether they are para-normal or human, we consider it our duty to protect those who need it," Marc cut in. "We are not a large group, but large enough that anyone coming into our territory should know better than to kidnap a woman right from under our noses. We take that very seriously on its own. The rest of this?" Marc shook his head and growled softly. "Unac-ceptable."

"They've been dealing with the Goldfangs while they're looking for Crissy. It's been a mess." Faith slumped to the side and Aldric wrapped his arm around her shoulders, holding her close and trying to lend her some of his strength if she needed it. She tipped her head to his shoulder in seeming acknowledgment.

"So, let's see if I can boil it down," Lucy said, eyeing Aldric and her niece. Faith sat up and nodded.

"This Jesse Honeyford snatched Crissy and tried to grab Kaylee as well because he is Kaylee's sperm donor," Lucy raised an eyebrow and Faith nodded.

"That's right. We're not sure if Kaylee will be a mage or a wolf. We'll have to wait and see," Faith said.

Lucy hummed. "After nearly mowing them all down, he did manage to grab Kaylee, along with your son Jake," Lucy glanced at Marc who nodded. She looked over out the window to the kids, both cheerfully running around the playset as three Enforcers watched-- both the kids and the surroundings-- with indulgent smiles. Kaylee yelled something and Ori started to cackle, nodding enthusiastically.

"Then, when you rescued the kids and found Crissy, she got snatched again in the middle of a battle with an unknown foe. After the dust from that has barely settled, you hear a rumor of wolves nearby with a captive, and you go to find them in the hopes that the captive is Crissy and find wolves *and* unknown vampires working together now, instead of against each other."

"That about sums it up. The captive wasn't Crissy, but Honeyford's younger brother who is, apparently, the only other person that Honeyford actually seems to care about. Jesse, I mean. He was livid to hear that his brother was taken and beaten to try to learn where Kaylee and Faith were hiding. Greg Honeyford had us take him to the cells once he had healed up enough and tore into his brother for the initial kidnapping situation, and stormed out again, without letting Jesse respond" Marc said. "That guy looks like a preschool teacher, all soft and sweet, but boy is he not at all soft when it comes down to it. He's going to teach the kids here this coming school year so we can keep them under guard more easily."

"And you trust him?"

"We do," Faith said. "He was in really bad shape, Aunt Lucy. And when he recovered enough for us to tell him what happened, he felt horribly guilty. I'll introduce you in a bit if you want, so you can interrogate him." Faith grinned. When Aldric raised a brow at her she giggled. "Maybe you could send Aunt Faith down to the cells to get a few more answers. Bet she comes back with information Ken missed."

"We will consider it," Aldric said, amused.

Faith sobered again after a breath and turned back to her aunt, who sat regarding them with a raised brow and a small smile. Aldric hoped that meant she had forgiven him for his species.

"You really knew about our magic this whole time?" Faith asked, her voice smaller than Aldric had heard before.

Lucy's smile softened and she reached out a hand. Faith jumped up and ran around the coffee table to settle beside her aunt, who took both of Faith's hands in her own. "Your parents wanted to make sure that I was ready, in case I needed to do exactly what I did. They needed me to know, and frankly, I'm glad they warned me or I would have shrieked the first time I saw you levitate something, or Crissy lighting one of those damned candles she loved in high school."

Faith groaned. "I did wonder why you always stressed out about fire safety. We thought you were just really nervous about apartment fires."

Lucy snorted. "I was. I was raising two young idiots that thought fire was a toy."

"We did not!" Faith grumbled.

Aldric exchanged a glance with Marc.

"Well, since there seem to be no secrets here to worry about, we will take your things upstairs to a room and let you get settled in," Marc said. "I'm making chili for dinner tonight, and it will be ready about six. Anything you don't eat I should know about?"

"Not a thing, I'm easy to feed," Lucy smiled at him. "And I should thank you. Both of you, it seems." She nodded at Aldric. "For keeping at least two of my girls safe. Anything I can do to help, I'm at your service. I would like to talk to this Leo fellow if you think I can."

Aldric nodded. "I will let you know when he calls in later this evening," Aldric said. "He is likely asleep right now."

"Ah. Vampire hours." Lucy nodded solemnly, but her eyes sparkled when she looked at him again. "Much the same thing as hacker hours, I suppose. You let me know. For now, I think Faith and I have a lot to talk about. Why don't you show me to a room, dear, and we'll catch up on three weeks of missed calls, hmm?"

The raised eyebrow left nobody in the room with the impression that Faith would be seen again before dinner.

CHAPTER 5

"So I was thinking that today we'd talk a bit about joining magics." Ken slung his bag into an empty chair and sat heavily before reaching over to pour himself some coffee from the carafe at the end of the table. This was how they usually started these lessons. A long chat about theory or how much Faith already knew about something, then Ken's rambling explanations, then they would move to the other end of the table away from the coffee and snacks Faith brought downstairs to eat before practice.

Ken always went for the coffee first, groaning at the first sip. "God, that is so much better than the swill at the station. I think it's a law that cop coffee has to be barely potable."

The comment about coffee was also part of his routine and made Faith grin.

"Joining magics?" she asked.

"Yep." He took another sip and reached for a sandwich. "I remembered last night that you mentioned Kaylee and Jake trying to help you out at the lodge battle. I'm a bit mad at myself that I didn't remember sooner, frankly. This is pretty important stuff. Not basic, mind you, but nothing about your training makes any sort of logical sense anyway at this point. We're just jumping around a bit."

Faith grimaced. "Sorry."

"Nah." Ken waved her off. "Not your fault. Car accidents are unpredictable, kind of by definition. Don't apologize that your teachers couldn't finish your lessons when you were a kid."

Faith couldn't help but feel a dull ache of grief at his comment. He meant it kindly but losing both her parents when she was so young still hurt, even though Aunt Lucy had worked hard to make sure that she and Crissy were happy and loved.

"Anyhow. Joining magic is where two mages focus their powers to cast a bigger spell than either would be able to do alone. It's usually tricky to do unless the mages in question are very close. You and Crissy could probably do it easily enough. Kaylee had no trouble throwing her energy to you in that fight at the lodge."

"But what about Jake?" Faith remembered the sensation of two very bright sparks of power in her mind, helping to fuel her shields during the surprise attack that had cost them Crissy and the life of one of the Enforcers. "I'm not related to him, and back then I'd only known him a few days."

Ken nodded. "True, but kids are easier a bit. Probably because they need to be guided so much by their parents and teachers. Although, I had never heard of a mage joining up with a werewolf before. I'm honestly surprised by it."

"Aldric once told me that vampires and shifters can't cast magic spells because they *are* magic. Their life force is woven too closely with it to use outside their own body."

Ken nodded. "That makes sense, in a way. I suppose that since he hadn't shifted yet, his magic was more available. I wonder if he could do it now? Not that I would suggest testing the theory, I mean he's a kid, but it's something to think about."

Faith nodded, thinking. "Maybe Tamika or someone would be willing to try? They're adults and more than able to give consent."

Ken shrugged. "Maybe. Not something I'm worried about, since hopefully once we get your sister back you'll be heading home, safe and sound."

Faith was pretty sure that she, at least, *was* home now. She had already called to discuss subletting her apartment to a friend of hers due to the situation with Crissy and her landlord had been very understanding. He even said he'd send someone to go clean out her fridge, which was something she hadn't even thought of. Faith mentally cringed at the thought and hoped that whoever ended up with that job was paid well.

"So. I figured we could try a few things today so you know how to do it on purpose. We'll practice with little things, like your feather flight exercise, just so you can get a feel for it," Ken reached for another sandwich. "These are so good. A good roast beef sandwich is a thing of glory."

Faith grinned. "Roast venison, but I agree. They're tasty."

"Venison?" Ken sounded surprised.

Faith nodded. "Yep. Aldric goes hunting once a week or so and brings back the deer. Otherwise, he feeds on bagged blood." She knew she was poking the bear a little, but didn't care. Ken didn't like the Frostwalker clan for reasons that made sense in a way. Mages had been hunted nearly to extinction by vampires, and to a much lesser extent, by werewolves. Faith hadn't known about the paranormal roots of World War Two until Aldric had told her about them.

Ken had lost most of his family, not that he had been around to know it. Still. The wariness was one of the few lessons her parents had drilled into them, as well, though they hadn't mentioned other paranormals. Just that nobody could know that they had magic.

So, when Ken found out that she was a mage, and she was living with the Frostwalker Clan, Ken had almost had a stroke. He still wasn't very comfortable around the others, but he had at least stopped trying to talk her into moving away from the Clan House. Good thing, too, because she really didn't want to fight with her new friend.

"Least he's not feeding off of you," Ken grumbled. He finished his sandwich and washed it down with more coffee then stood. "Come on, let's get some practice in."

Faith nodded and grabbed a water bottle. This was going to be exhausting, she could tell.

"**O**h, sweet, sweet sofa. I'm going to live here, now." Faith tipped over and flopped onto the cushion of the couch in the den. It was not the one that the kids used for couch forts, since the cushions were overstuffed and yet perfectly smooshy, therefore not structurally sound enough for fortifications. They were, however exactly what Faith wanted after the grueling practice Ken had marched her through. She took a small amount of satisfaction in seeing that he looked a bit tired himself.

"It's hard work, magic. Takes practice, like any other exercise," he said, gesturing with the water bottle he held.

"You're the meanest personal trainer ever," Faith grumbled into the pillow.

"Your magic muscles are--"

"Oh, I'm sorry. Didn't mean to interrupt, but I saw Faith flop over as I headed to the kitchen and wanted to know what's wrong."

Ken stiffened and narrowed his eyes at Lucy, standing in the door. Faith didn't move except to flick her fingers vaguely in Ken's direction.

"Ken's been helping me learn more about my magic. And he's a cruel taskmaster," Faith felt no need to play nice here. That last hour was brutal, focusing on both keeping her connection to Ken's magic open while at the same time moving that damned feather in very specific patterns. "He is trying to kill me."

Lucy frowned. "I thought your mother taught you your magic?"

Ken scowled as well, but Faith could tell it was his confused-and-didn't-like-it scowl, not his angry scowl.

"Ken, this is my aunt Lucy. She raised us, and apparently, knew that we could do magic the whole time." Faith waved her hand toward her aunt and then let it drop back onto the couch.

"Sit up, Faith. There's no call for poor manners no matter how tired and lazy you're feeling." Lucy nudged Faith's knee, then when Faith had levered herself upright again, plopped down to sit next to her. Faith settled for leaning on her aunt's shoulder.

"It's nice to meet you, Ken. You're the detective who is looking into Crissy's disappearance?"

Ken nodded, his scowl had softened slightly at the introduction. "I am, though since she was taken by non-humans, there is only so much I can do, professionally speaking," His scowl deepened again. "I hate to say that these people are better equipped to raid another paranormal's hideout, but I can't take a human SWAT team in to fight a nest of vampires."

Lucy pursed her lips and nodded. "Agreed. We don't want a massacre."

"It galls me to say that," Ken growled. "I hate relying on these... *people* for lack of a better word. Creatures is closer, but insulting to normal animals everywhere."

Faith glanced at her aunt who had raised an eyebrow.

"You don't like the Frostwalkers?" Lucy asked.

"Detective Lincoln has a relatively understandable reluctance to trust vampires," a new voice said. "I believe werewolves have been put into the same category out of an abundance of caution." Uncle Eldridge stepped into the room and dipped his head in greeting.

"Caution my ass," Ken sputtered and surged to his feet. "You people *hunted* us for *food!* Entire families, including the children, were eaten by you power-hungry leeches! It's a damn miracle that there are any of us left!"

Eldridge simply stood there, a mild expression on his face, and let Ken snarl at him.

"Young man, sit down," Lucy's voice cracked through the air and Faith almost cringed. She knew that tone and half expected that she'd end the conversation grounded for a week, even though it hadn't been directed at her. "Do you even hear yourself, Detective?"

Oh, dear. Aunt Lucy used his title. It was probably a good thing that she didn't know Ken's middle name, too.

"I know exactly what I'm saying, and you should be listening. Help me get Faith and Kaylee away from these people and somewhere safe!" Ken turned imploring eyes on Lucy. "They're as good as prisoners here, just as much as they'd be with the other group. They're in danger, too!"

"They are locked in a room? Fed stale sandwiches? They have their movements constrained?" Lucy raised her brow again. "I would say that they have rather more freedom here than they probably ought to, all things considered. There are, indeed, people hunting them. I'd keep them in heavily guarded rooms well inside the house until Crissy is found and these people are dealt with, but instead, the Frostwalkers are working very hard to keep my girls safe while letting them live as normal a life as possible. Kaylee plays outside and I understand she and Jake are going swimming this afternoon. I also understand that Aldric has arranged for twice as many bodyguards as normal to accompany them, to the pool, as well as Marc himself going along. that's not how anyone treats a prisoner."

"Then let them go stay somewhere else if these Frost-walkers are so selfless!" Ken growled at Eldridge., then swung back around to Lucy "They won't allow that, will they? Their precious *paranormal priorities* won't let them leave Faith and Kaylee alone! Then you mark my words, those vamps will be using Faith like a damn energy drink!"

"Oh don't be an ass," Lucy said. "I heard enough of that sort bigoted horseshit when my brother David started dating Jennifer, except then it was about Asians. You don't have any right to judge anyone, Detective. Stop living in the past and look at the allies you have in the present."

Eldridge cleared his throat. "To be entirely fair to the detective, most of the humans who fought in that war have passed away. Many of the werewolves and vampires who fought back then are still alive and well." He paused. "Myself and Aldric included."

"You two fought in World War Two?" Both of Lucy's brows rose now, and Faith watched, amused, as her aunt stared at Eldridge. Her eyes widened slightly and a small blush rose in the cheek Faith could see.

Not that Faith could blame Lucy. Where Aldric had dark brown hair and broad shoulders, Eldridge was fair and slim like a swimmer, but they both had the same mossy green eyes, and both could easily find space in the glossy pages of fashion magazines.

"We did," Eldridge nodded while Ken sputtered and fumed quietly. "Our family has always lived and worked alongside the Magaestra, and to see them hunted and used like that was not something we could stand back and ignore. Aldric and I were among the first to sign up to fight with the other paranormals trying to contain the situation. Then later when the humans became embroiled in the war as well, Aldric and I joined the American army while Aldric's father continued working for the paranormal forces. My children both worked as medics, and our wives both helped organize extraction and concealment for any of the human mages we could find."

"That's amazing. I don't believe I've met the rest of your family," Lucy said. Faith tried not to laugh.

"I can't listen to this," Ken stood up and stormed toward the hallway.

"Detective," Lucy called. "I do hope that you will think, once you've calmed down. Use that mind of yours to consider your reactions. Are the Frostwalkers really as bad as you say, or are you judging them on the actions of some villains from long ago?"

Ken snarled and stomped out the door. Eldridge tipped his head, listening, until he shrugged, ruefully. "He has left the Clan House. I'm sorry for interrupting and possibly making the situation worse."

"Not at all," Lucy waved his arguments away. Now, you are Aldric's uncle, I think I've heard? Do I get to meet your wife and children, as well?"

CHAPTER 6

Aldric glanced over at Faith and spent a few minutes watching the rise and fall of her chest. She had come in some hour and a half earlier grumbling about Detective Lincoln's biases and something about-- Aldric was sure he heard wrong-- her aunt Lucy and his uncle Eldridge flirting in the den. She then plopped down on the sofa and pulled the blanket over herself and said she was going to take a damn nap and nobody could stop her. That she sought him out just so he could stand guard over her while she slept... *I will not fail her again* he promised himself.

A beep from his computer brought his attention back to his desk, and he clicked the *accept call* button quickly, hoping the noise didn't wake Faith.

"Woah, hey cuz. That goofy smile thing you've got going on is a good look for you. I take it Faith's around?" Leo's voice held laughter and his eyes sparkled.

"Keep your voice down," Aldric shushed his cousin. "Faith is napping on the sofa and I do not wish to wake her."

Leo's expression softened, and he spoke more softly when he answered. "Sorry, Aldric."

"Thank you, Now, what have you learned that you are calling me for?"

Leo grinned again. "Well, it's not much, really, but it's a lead. Addison-- you remember Addison? She came back to town when she heard about the whole mess, and says that if she needs to take a family emergency leave from the university next semester she will. Anyway, Addison dug up this old mine map from the county archives."

Aldric blinked. "A mine map? This is progress?"

"I'd guess it's connected to that cave we landed in last week." Faith's voice was still thick with sleep, but she was sitting up on the sofa, stretching.

"Oh! I'm sorry I woke you up, Faith. Good morning!" Leo spoke a bit louder again.

She smiled and shook herself for a moment before answering. "Hardly morning at four-thirty P.M., but thanks." Faith walked over and leaned on Aldric's shoulder to peer at the screen, and he soaked up the warmth where she touched him. Vampires weren't cold to the touch like so many novels would claim. They were not undead, or cursed, or anything like that. They were simply a different, near-human species that happened to be at least in part animated by magic and required liquid blood as a part of their diet.

He still wanted to wrap Faith's warmth around himself like a blanket. He settled for reaching his hand up to cover hers where it rested on his shoulder.

"So what about this mine map is so interesting?" she asked

"Well, we found where it used to come out in that little camp that we raided. That cave used to be a mine entrance using a natural opening in the ground that was expanded and shored up, it looks like. The building over it was originally used to keep the rain out to prevent flooding of the equipment. If there'd been any light down there I'd guess you would have seen rainwater channels in the cave proper, too." Leo clicked on something and glanced at a different screen. "We've only digitized part of it so far. These tunnels are a freaking maze, with levels and twisty parts that overlap on each other... It's a bit of a mess. Addison is scanning as fast as she can and then trying to clean up the images, but it's slow going. These maps are almost as old as you are, Aldric, and not very carefully done."

"So what are you thinking?" Aldric asked. "What has you so excited to find these maps?"

Faith laced her fingers through Aldric's and he had to force his attention back to his cousin.

"Well, I think that door you saw leads somewhere. And considering that those lunatics had the place rigged to blow, I'd guess it's somewhere they didn't want anyone knowing about." Leo raised an eyebrow at his camera.

"You think they were using it as, what? An escape tunnel?" Faith asked.

"I think they were using it to move people and supplies unseen," Leo said. "We've all been looking for places where there's been an uptick in activity, but if it gets spread out over several state park entrances then it would less likely for us to notice it. The fact that this place was so close to the Frostwalker Clan House and all our people..."

They sat with that thought for a moment before Faith spoke up. "That is some super-secret spy crap, right there."

Leo snorted and Aldric smiled.

"But the good news is that once we sort out these maps, we can trace the possible paths in and out, and maybe come up with an idea of where the rest of these jerks are based," Leo said. "And once we know that, hopefully, we'll know where to look for Crissy. Addison is almost done scanning all the bits in, and once we've got them cleaned up we'll send them to you, too. More eyes means more chances of catching something. I just wanted to make sure you know this was coming your way. Give us, like, twelve hours or so to get it all cleaned up."

"Thanks, Leo," Faith said.

"I will expect to hear from you soon, Leo. I am eager to locate Crissy and end this," Aldric agreed.

"I'm just glad we finally found something. It was no wonder I missed it: it was all physical maps in boxes in a dusty backroom," Leo grinned. "I knew she was good with computers, but I had no idea Addison's American history minor was going to come in so damn handy! Catch you guys later!"

There was a click, then the image of Leo disappeared, and they were left staring at the scheduling spreadsheet Aldric had been working on for the Enforcer patrols. Faith pointed out an error in one of the columns but didn't move, so Aldric pushed away from the desk and tugged her down into his lap.

"We will find her. We haven't stopped looking." He wrapped his arms loosely around her waist as she laid her head down on his shoulder and just sort of slumped into his arms.

"I know," she said. "I know that. I'm just... It's been weeks, Aldric. I'm scared and so damn tired."

He nodded and lowered his head to kiss her hair, then rested his cheek against the same place. "Then rest. Let us take the burden for you a while."

"I feel a bit selfish letting you do that. But at the same time..." She sniffled. "Thank you, Aldric. I don't think I could have gotten this far without you. Assuming we even survived that first attack, which I doubt we would have, I'd probably have sent Kaylee off to Aunt Lucy in L.A. and then gotten myself kidnapped, too, and then..."

Aldric stroked up her spine, trying to take the sad, resigned tone out of her voice.

"But you didn't. You not only survived that initial attempt, but you gathered allies. You have gained resources and training. I know that you are working with Tamika on self-defense and with Detective Lincoln to improve your magical skills. You bake cookies and cupcakes with the children to keep their spirits up, and I believe you and Greg were discussing how to set up a small private school of some sort for the children, so they will not fall behind should they be unable to return to classes in the fall."

Faith chuckled. "It's not that long from now, even. School starts in like, two weeks or something. End of August."

Aldric frowned. "That feels very early."

Faith shrugged but didn't move, causing her shoulder to rub up and down his chest and her head to bump gently against his chin. "I don't make the rules. I just complain about them later. I already pulled Kaylee from her old preschool. They were very understanding and were pleased to know that she visited Mr. Greg after he was rescued. It means that we're less likely to sue them for whatever since he was working for them when all this started."

Aldric nodded. "So you've said."

"But really," she pulled back a bit to peer up at him. "Thank you. I'd be a mess without you."

Aldric smiled. "It is my honor."

Faith smiled up at him and stretched up to kiss him. Aldric silently thanked any god that might be listening and let her.

CHATPER 7

Faith tugged the ties on her robe and tried not to be weird about sniffing the snuggly collar. It still smelled like Aldric, which made sense since he lent it to her, but she'd been wearing it for almost a month now so the fact that the scent was still so strong was a bit surprising. Not that Faith was going to complain. She peeked into Kaylee's room and sighed when she didn't see the girl curled up in her bed.

Faith took a few steps down the hall and poked her nose into Jake's room and sighed again, seeing the trundle bed pulled out and two kids and a handful of stuffies sprawled across the mattress. It was sweet that Jake was so protective and affectionate towards Kaylee, but they were getting old enough that the sleepovers were going to have to stop.

"They're pretty cute, all cuddled up, huh?" Aunt Lucy said from behind Faith.

"Yeah. But they're getting bigger. And eventually, we'll get Crissy back. Who knows where we'll live once that happens." Faith pulled the door almost closed again and headed back towards her own room. "I just wanted to check in on her before I settled into bed."

Lucy chuckled as she followed. "I know the feeling. That girl is no better at staying where she's supposed to than you were at her age. I heard about her little adventure in evading her bodyguards."

"She's never been in a situation where it was dangerous to wander around her own home." Faith dug a new t-shirt out of the clean laundry she hadn't put away yet. Wonder Woman again. She could use a spot of Amazon Princess confidence. The longer this dragged out the more tense she got. It was starting to feel almost too heavy for her to stand.

Aunt Lucy didn't respond, just wandered a bit around her room, peering at the pictures on the walls that Faith hadn't picked out and the rocks and leaves and dried flowers she had on her dresser that she hadn't picked out either, but were gifts from the kids. Aunt Lucy got to the bedside table and picked up one of the books, reading the back and raising an eyebrow at Faith who grinned.

"Why yes, it is a vampire romance novel," Faith's grin widened and she felt lighter. "Aldric lent it to me."

Lucy chuckled and shook her head as she put it back down. "That young man is quite a refreshing change from your usual type."

"My usual type?" Faith frowned at her aunt.

"Yeah. Emotionally distant or stunted." Lucy sat on the bed and looked at her. "You seem to have spent most of your life actively avoiding men with whom you could form any sort of emotional bond. Aldric is, as far as I can tell, very nearly an open book."

Faith sat beside her aunt and frowned, this time in thought. Looking back she could sort of see what Lucy meant. Most of her exes were... not very forthcoming. They were masculine in that *I can't even admit I have feelings, let alone talk about them* sort of way. Aldric was not even slightly like that. And yet, he managed to be entirely too male.

"I don't seek out emotionally stunted men..." Faith frowned

Lucy raised an eyebrow. "Now I know I haven't met all your dates, but the ones I have met... do you remember James? And Franklin? And Kyle?"

"Okay, that's not fair. Kyle was back in high school. Come on!" Faith protested, but she was starting to think that Aunt Lucy was right.

Lucy laughed. "Look, I'm not trying to get on your case about your past taste in men. I just wanted to check in with you and see where you are in your head with this one. It's a hell of a high-emotion time to get involved with anyone."

Faith nodded her agreement. "Yeah. I just... I feel safe with him. And I don't have to put up any sort of front around him, you know? He's seen me at my absolute worst already. I mean, I've had moments of seriously ugly crying on his shoulder, and he still wants me around. He *blushes* Luce. I didn't know guys did that in real life!"

Lucy smiled. "I'm glad to hear that. And I'm also glad to hear that you can relax around him. He seems a reliable sort of fellow. And handsome." Lucy wiggled her eyebrows at Faith.

Faith smirked. "Mmmm. Both those things seem to run in the family. I did notice you and Eldridge chatting all the way through dinner."

Aunt Lucy laughed. "Eldridge is certainly handsome— I'm old, not dead. He has some wonderful stories."

Faith grinned. The women chatted for another hour

before Faith's yawns were cracking her jaw and Lucy raised an eyebrow at her. "Do I need to tuck you in to make sure you go to bed, young lady?"

"Only if you make me some warm milk first! With vanilla and cinnamon!" Faith laughed. "You know Crissy makes that for Kaylee all the time? I had to teach the guys here how to make it 'the right way' according to her, and now Jake has it most nights, too. And Marc and Aldric. And I think half the Enforcers."

Lucy chuckled. "It is tough to beat. There's just something about that touch of spice."

Faith grinned. "Marc said it was just enough Christmas in the summer to make his heart feel warm, too." Her own heart squeezed and her smile faded. "Crissy would love that. That whole idea."

"Oh, sweetheart. You'll get to tell her." Lucy wrapped her arms around Faith and pulled her close, and Faith soaked up the feeling of *family* and *Aunt Lucy* and being held by the woman that raised her.

"What happens if I don't get to tell her?" Faith whispered. "What if it's too late already? It's been nearly a month! Even though she seemed to be fine when we saw her at the lodge, that was still weeks ago, and we all know what those vampires want us for, and it's not a tropical vacation."

Lucy sighed, her breath brushing over Faith's hair. "Oh, sweetheart. If it's too late then we do our best to carry on. We mourn, and we raise Kaylee and keep her mother's memory alive for her and teach her everything she'll need to know to survive in the world. You won't be alone though. You have me, and you have the Frostwalker Clan. Marc and Aldric and the rest of them would never let you do it all on your own like I had to."

"How did you do it? How did you keep me and Crissy from crying all the time?" Faith sniffled. "I remember when you came. The babysitter called a neighbor over and she stayed with us all night but nobody would tell us what was going on or where Mom and Dad were. And then you showed up in the morning and the neighbor cried, and you sniffled, but you looked right at us, sitting at the breakfast table in our pajamas, and smiled."

"It was probably the worst day of my whole life. Well, it was until you told me about Crissy. I cried all the way across the country in that plane. I know I worried the flight attendants. I lost my brother and my best friend both at the same time. But you girls needed me to be strong enough for you to fall apart for a while."

"I've been trying so hard to stay strong for Kaylee. It's so hard."

Lucy leaned down to press a kiss to her forehead and looked her in the eye. "It is. It's sometimes impossibly hard. But as I said, you are not alone. I couldn't lean on anyone for fear that they would discover your secret. You have a whole clan of paranormals around you to help, and that Ken fellow, grumpy as he is. I know he fusses and argues about it, but if he was completely irredeemable, he wouldn't come up here at all. You have me, and I know some of what you're going through. You've got this, honey."

Faith let Lucy hold her, rocking them both slightly as if she was a child in need of reassurance. It was so hard, way harder than she had expected, to be Kaylee's parental figure. She didn't like to dwell on it, and Kaylee was generally a pretty easy kid, but they hadn't had a 100% smooth time of it this summer. Some lashing out was expected, and honestly reasonable.

Kaylee hated that they were effectively under siege in

the Clan House. They weren't going for hikes or swims in the creek, or to the movies, or out for ice cream without a whole platoon of bodyguards— none of the things that were normally such a huge part of coming up to the cabin. The farthest that she could go outside was the playset, and that was only if there were three or more guards with them.

Thank all that was holy for Jake. That kid was a hero and didn't even know it. He worked every day to keep Kaylee cheerful. And now that Mr. Greg was here and mostly headed up, he had taken to doing projects with both kids in the mornings, keeping them both entertained and sneakily teaching them. Faith hadn't wanted to like the guy after his role in accidentally outing the Latham's to his brother, but he had officially joined the Frostwalkers and sworn an oath of loyalty to Marc, the Clan, and the Frostwalker's ideals of family, community, and responsibility.

He had also spent nearly an hour calmly and verbally taking his brother apart in the most vicious schoolteacher sort of way. He had limped down to the holding cells before he had finished healing, the bruises and welts still making an ugly pattern across his body, determined to confront his brother. Faith wouldn't have believed that Jesse Honeyford was even capable of remorse or regret, but the man was cringing within minutes and had been subdued and as helpful as he was able to be since that afternoon.

Kaylee still had nightmares and, like tonight, more often than not ended up in Jake's room in a puppy pile. Faith had no idea how to keep the girl in her own bed, and it was going to be a problem eventually, but for now, she and Marc had made the parental decision that it was probably okay. Kaylee was traumatized and had decided that Jake was her safe person, and Jake, bless the boy, had more than risen to the challenge.

"What am I going to do?" Faith asked. "I feel really selfish, but even without Kaylee, I need my sister. And then I go to Aldric and find this... this *peace* and I can smile and laugh and then I come back here and feel so damn guilty for not being out there looking for Crissy. For not spending all my time searching."

"You can't help her if you don't take care of yourself, Faith," Aunt Lucy said, not pausing her slow back and forth and running her hand over Faith's hair. "Kaylee found her solace in Jake. You have found yours in Aldric. There is no shame in that, and you shouldn't feel guilty about it, either."

"And what if it was vampires that have kept Crissy this whole time? What if they've been..." Faith whispered. She didn't want to say it out loud.

"Your sister is undoubtedly going to be traumatized when we get her back. But that won't be Aldric's fault. or Eldridge's. Or Leo and Madeline's fault. I know that those four have been working their fangs off to find Crissy and she'll understand that, too. Eventually. You said that she met Aldric briefly during the first rescue attempt?"

Faith nodded.

"And did she seem afraid of him then?"

Faith shrugged. "Wary, for sure. She didn't trust him at all, but she could tell that Kaylee and I did. And Jake. So she didn't argue too much."

Aunt Lucy nodded and pulled back. "Then she also knows that he's been working with you to find her. When we do get her back she will have a lot of work to do, and thank goodness this Clan has a few therapists among them. But I believe that it will all work out."

"Especially if it turns out that Kaylee is a shifter and not a mage," Faith chuckled damply. She reached up and felt the tears she hadn't even noticed spilling, and scrubbed her hand over her cheeks to dry them.

"It will all work out, sweetheart," Aunt Lucy said, smiling slightly and reaching for the tissue box on the nightstand. "I have faith."

Faith groaned, but she did feel better. A little.

CHAPTER 8

The knocking on his door woke Aldric instantly. He had been sleeping very lightly for the past few weeks, half expecting an attack at any moment, and being woken like this at-- he peered at his alarm clock-- four oh seven a.m. had his adrenaline rushing. The knock repeated.

"Aldric!" Marc's voice carried a note of urgency, but Aldric couldn't hear any sounds of fighting.

"I'm awake, what it is?" he pulled the door open to find his friend fully dressed with his cell phone pressed to his ear.

"Get dressed. I need you to head to the clinic," Marc's face twisted with anger. "Detective Lincoln was attacked in his home."

"What?" Aldric left the door open and hurried to his dresser to pull out some pants. Marc followed him in and paced.

"We really ought to have seen it coming, honestly. He is also a mage, after all, and these people seem to be collecting them, just like they did eighty years ago," Marc growled. "We should have had him assigned guards."

Aldric sat to lace up his boot. "Do you truly believe Detective Lincoln would have allowed us to send bodyguards with him everywhere? He is far too independent and stubborn, as well, he doesn't exactly trust us due to his bias." Aldric stood and grabbed his jacket. "I am going armed. Before I go, I will wake Tamika and tell her what has happened, and have her check in with the sentries here. I will call Kenya and Ori to go investigate Detective Lincoln's house, and contact you as soon as I have information."

"He's as stable and as comfortable as I can get him, but despite the fact that you have been using this place as an emergency room and trauma center for the past few weeks, we are not actually a hospital. I have a transport coming for him in the next couple of hours to take him into the city where they can make sure that he's okay. He's human, and I want to run tests that I don't have the equipment for." Madeline sighed over her desk. "I'll take you to see him in a minute, but Aldric..." she shook her head.

"I know. This has to end." Aldric frowned and shook his head. "Leo believes that he has a lead on how to locate the base these vampires are operating out of. With a little luck, this will be over soon."

"Assuming that finding their local base of operations will solve the problem," Madeline said. "I think at this point we all know that they're after humans with magic, and the only way to stop them is to find out who's stirring them up and stop that person."

Aldric grimaced. She was correct, after all. They needed to find the head of this monster and cut it off there. If the paranormal community had sanctioned the Immortal Thirst coven and its Master before he got so power mad that he sent his people out to actively hunt and collect mages in the first place, a great deal of violence and brutality could likely have been prevented.

"Let me see Lincoln," he said instead. There was nothing he could do about the larger problem at the moment.

"He's not really awake. I've got him pretty heavily sedated so if he does talk to you it isn't likely to make any sense."

Aldric nodded and followed his cousin. She led him to the small room that he himself had been in not too long ago. On the bed lay Detective Lincoln, pale and somehow smaller than he truly was. His breathing seemed loud against the quiet of the early morning hours in the clinic, and he had a tube running over his face that Aldric assumed was providing the man with oxygen.

"He's got a couple of broken bones, a ton of nasty bruises, a concussion, and I don't like the wheezing although I don't think it's anything *too* scary. That and the head injury are the main reasons I called the transport." Madeline grimaced. "And he doesn't have our healing abilities, so I can't in good conscience treat him here."

"I ran my batteries out, s'all," Lincoln grumbled, his words not as crisp as they usually were. "Fuckin' vamps thought I'd go easy."

"They were foolish, then. I would never have made that assumption. Even without magic, you are not the sort to allow yourself to be abducted," Aldric agreed. "Can you tell me what happened?"

"There will be police here soon as well. I have to call them or they'll start to investigate me. Fair warning," Madeline said before slipping out the door. "I will tell them that he was being treated and couldn't answer questions, but they will undoubtedly send someone over anyway."

"With luck, it'll be Steven," Aldric said, and Madeline nodded, pulling the door almost closed. "He already knows what's going on."

"So, Detective, what happened?" Aldric pulled a chair up beside the bed between the detective and the door and sat.

"Sleeping. Assholes busted in my door. Dunno how they got through the wards though," Lincoln frowned and sucked in another breath. "I got a warning that they were breached, an' then the vamps were bustin' in my door. First two got fireballs to the face." He snickered, then coughed.

Aldric nodded. "Good. I must apologize, Detective. I feel this was my fault. I should have assigned some sentries to watch over you."

Lincoln scoffed. "I can take carea myself." His words were slurring together more now and his eyelids drooped.

"I am fully aware. But you do not need to defend yourself alone. I have spoken to Tamika and she is sending over two sentries to act as your bodyguards while you recover."

"Don't need—"

"Please. For our sake," Aldric said. Then he added, "For Faith's peace of mind."

Lincoln started to sigh but it turned into a cough. "Fine."

They sat for a moment, Aldric watching the detective breathe.

"I think I got all of 'em. Crispy vamps. Like steaks." Detective Lincoln giggled. "Vampire stakes. 'S funny. Get it?" His giggle turned into a cough again and Aldric gently laid a hand on his arm.

"I sent Ori and Kenya to your home to investigate. With luck they can get the remains out of your house before the police arrive there," Aldric said. "And I will stay here until your transport arrives. Your guards will go with you."

Lincoln didn't answer out loud, just blinked at Aldric. He nodded slightly, and his eyes drifted closed.

Aldric watched the detective breathe for a long time, before he sat back with a sigh, scrubbed his fingers through his hair, and pulled out his phone to start texting.

CHAPTER 9

Faith yawned so wide that she felt her jaw pop. It was six-thirty in the morning, a completely normal time to wake up for most people, but she had gotten somewhat used to sleeping in a little and then wandering into the kitchen around eight when Marc was flipping another batch of pancakes or making more waffles or something for the adults to eat after he fed the kids. This morning, however, something has woken her. A gut feeling that all was not well.

She stumbled into the kitchen, wondering if Marc was up yet, and found a half-full coffee pot that was still hot, but no Marc. Once she had her mug of morning wake-up fuel, she wandered into the hallway where the offices were, wondering if she could find anyone up.

"-- then I guess you should stay there until it gets sorted out. I don't want him unguarded." Marc was on the phone, scowling so hard at his computer that she was impressed that it wasn't cowering.

She stepped quietly into the room and sat down in one

of the armchairs in front of his desk and sipped her coffee while she waited. Marc glanced over and his gaze softened slightly.

"Yeah. I'll tell Faith. She just walked in, actually, do you want to-- Yeah, okay." Marc pulled the phone away from his head and held it out to Faith. "I hope you're awake enough to talk to Aldric. He could use a friendly voice. Hell, I could too."

"Uh," Faith reached out and took the phone. "Hello? Aldric?"

"Faith. Good morning." Aldric sounded exhausted. "At least I hope your morning is good. Mine has been stressful."

"What happened? Where are you?" Faith was pretty sure she hadn't had enough coffee yet and gulped down most of what she had poured. Marc copied her action then stood and silently held his hand out to take her mug.

"I'm at the clinic right now. I should have been home an hour ago to report to Marc, but the hospital transport met with a gruesome accident that I suspect was far from accidental." His tired sigh came through the handset. "I have spent the past forty minutes organizing a secure transport from here to the nearest hospital. I..."

"Who's hurt? What's going on?" Faith asked. Marc came back into the room and handed her a fresh cup.

"I started a new pot," he said and sat down.

"I am sorry to tell you this. Detective Lincoln was attacked in his home very early this morning. He successfully fought off the vampires who broke into his house and managed to call Marc since calling an ambulance would have required far too many explanations. As it is we had to do some fast talking as to why that was when his police colleagues arrived here."

"I'll be there in twenty minutes." Faith stood up and started to hurry out of the room when Aldric stopped her.

"Faith, no. I need to know that you are safe at the house. Kaylee also. You know full well that you are targets. I should have had sentries watching over Detective Lincoln as it was. I should have known that these people would go after him, not only as our ally but because he is also..." Aldric's voice trailed off as someone started speaking in the background. "Faith, I must go. Stay there, and tell Marc I will call back when there is more information, or in an hour, whichever comes first."

"Aldric!" Faith tried to stop him, but the call cut off. "Goddamnit."

She scowled at the phone for a moment before handing it back. "He'll call back later."

Marc grunted.

"Okay, Marc. What happened?" Faith narrowed her eyes at him, determined to get as many details as she could.

Marc sighed and grimaced. "I only know what I was just told. This morning at around four I got a garbled phone call from Detective Lincoln. He was clear enough to let me know that he was injured and needed medical help but was reluctant to call an ambulance due to the charred remains of two vampires and a few blighthounds."

"*What?*" Faith was half out of her seat, about to run upstairs and grab some clothes.

"So I called Madeline who took one of the sentries assigned to the clinic and went to get Lincoln and take him for treatment. Then I woke Aldric, who headed over as well. Detective Lincoln has got several claw wounds, a not very deep bite from a hound, a concussion, and probably some bruising on his lungs, though apparently, Madeline doesn't think he cracked any ribs." Marc shook his head and took a deep breath to continue.

"That's one reason Madeline wanted to send him to the city. Their x-ray equipment is better than hers is here. He did break his left wrist, though, and might need surgery to make sure it heals right. Aldric says that he's pretty pale and drained-looking, which I assume is from heavy magic use," he said. "There were two very crispy vampires and one half-burned blighthound corpse, with evidence that another hound ran off, injured. Ori went to track down the injured hound and Kenya handled cleaning up the bodies before the police descended there. But that's not what Aldric just called about." Now he sat back and scowled at his phone

Faith's knees dropped her back into the chair when they gave up. "There's more?"

Marc sucked in a deep breath. "Yeah. Madeline called a medical transport so that Lincoln could get taken to an actual hospital-- and let me tell you, I got an earful this morning about how the clinic is not an emergency room nor is it a trauma center, and if we are going to treat it like one we need to pay for renovations and buy her a ton of equipment, *and* find another doctor we trust to treat paranormals."

Faith nodded. They had been leaning hard on Madeline this summer. It wasn't anyone here's fault that a paranormal skirmish had broken out in the area, and the wolves-- and Aldric-- needed to be treated by someone that wouldn't freak out about their rapid healing. Still, Madeline was right that there was only so much she was equipped to deal with.

"Anyway, the transport was run off the road on the way here," Marc said. He met Faith's gaze and the anxiety and determination and anger in his eye made her shiver.

"Is everyone okay?" she asked. She wasn't sure she wanted to know the answer.

"No." Marc didn't elaborate. He did start growling though. "Aldric has alerted Tamika and Rod, and the Enforcers are each calling the sentries that they supervise. The whole clan is going on high alert. I was going to come to wake you when I got off the phone. Our whole security force is scrambling right now, and our phone tree is buzzing with warnings of possible hostile forces in the area."

"*Possible* hostile forces?" Faith blinked. There seemed to be nothing *possible* about it!

"Okay, you're right." Marc nodded in agreement. "Definitely hostile and definitely in the area. They've been poking around for some time, but this is the most blatant attack yet, going after an ambulance and medical personnel that aren't even involved in any of this. Cops are swarming over Detective Lincoln's house now. Kenya barely got out herself. Madeline and Aldric have had officers buzzing all over the clinic, too, and I guarantee I am going to hear about *that* from her when this is all dealt with, too."

Faith sat back, her mind buzzing with all this information. Marc scowled at his computer screen and poked a few keys before hitting backspace angrily.

"I'm still going to the clinic," Faith said and stood up. "Ken needs another mage around if he's as drained as you say. And Aldric is going to need the moral support."

"Faith, I can't let you run off like that. It's too dangerous to be out there right now." Marc stood and came around the desk. "I understand your desire to help, and I can't thank you enough for being the sort of person who rushes to help rather than to run and hide, but in this specific case, I need to overrule you. I need to know exactly where everyone is right now and keep movement to a minimum. Even Kenya and Ori are hunkered down at this point. Tamika's in Aldric's office trying to organize the search for where the vamps that attacked Lincoln came from and where the hound went after it got away from Ori. Leo is hunting down any possible evidence on traffic cameras, but since it happened at around the halfway point on the freeway, he's not very optimistic."

Marc reached out and gripped her shoulders, his fingers squeezing a bit to reassure her. "We are doing everything we can to sort this out already, and the second I think it's safe for you to head over there, I'll drive you myself. But we don't know where the ambushers went, or if there are more out there waiting for us. So for right now, we need everyone to stay put. Please."

Faith growled but didn't say anything. Marc knew she wouldn't go alone-- she wasn't entirely stupid-- and if he had ordered everyone to stay put, then she was stuck. He was the chief of the Frostwalker Clan, and that gave him the authority to give the order, and that left her stuck.

Marc squeezed her shoulders lightly and tried to smile reassuringly, but it looked too tired and stressed to be more than a grimace. So, she stepped back and turned, and headed out the door, grumbling.

"Thank you, Faith!" Marc's called out after her. "I'll keep you updated!"

"Right!" she called back, not slowing down. She wasn't even sure where she was going, but she couldn't stand there and glare at Marc for long. She needed to move. Ken was hurt. Aldric was out there in who knew how much danger. And she was expected to just hide at home, like a good little damsel.

She turned the corner and slammed right into a hard chest.

"Woah there, everything okay?" Frankie rumbled.

"There were attacks overnight. Ken was hurt. Everyone's stuck where they are because Marc wants to sort this mess out before anyone does anything else. So, I can't get to the clinic to see Ken or Aldric," Faith practically snarled the last part. "Men!"

Frankie scrunched up his face. "I'm sure that they're just trying to keep everyone safe."

Faith didn't appreciate the placating tone in his voice. "I'm not exactly a helpless idiot, you know. I can handle myself."

Frankie chuckled at that. "I've seen you in the training sessions with Tamika. I believe you."

They had reached the staircase in the front hall now. Faith sighed. She was being unreasonable and she damn well knew it, but Ken needed her. She knew that, too.

"Look," Frankie started to say something, then stopped. Faith turned to look at him and he was staring pensively back toward the corner that led to the offices. Something in his eyes flickered and he seemed to come to a decision.

"I know what it feels like to be left out of the action when someone you care about is in the thick of it. So, I'm not saying anything, you know, but if someone happened to wander out past the garage and toward the overflow parking, it's possible that someone might be able to head out and drive somewhere from there." Frankie shrugged. "In say, ten minutes."

Faith blinked. "Why would *someone* do that?" She had to ask.

Frankie blinked and his gaze shifted. Now he wasn't looking at anything that she could see. He was remembering something or someone, and it hurt.

"Because I know what love feels like," he said quietly.

"Oh," she couldn't think of anything else to say. It was very clear that the memory hurt, deeply. There was a story there, she knew, but now wasn't the time to ask. "Thank you." She put her hand on his arm and stretched up to peck a kiss to his cheek. "I'll get dressed. I think I feel like wandering around a bit. In say, ten minutes."

Frankie just nodded and sent her a stiff smile as she turned to dash up the stairs.

CHAPTER 10

What a damned awful morning. Aldric slumped in his seat, his head dropping forward to rest on the wheel for a moment before he dragged himself inside to Marc's office. All he wanted was to find Faith and curl up somewhere and have a nap.

A tap on the window made him jump, and he glared at his friend when Marc grinned.

"Come on, man. You've been sitting out here for fifteen minutes," he said through the glass.

"I have?" Damn.

"I just made some coffee, and you should have a bag of blood. It's going to be a long day." Marc stepped back to let Aldric open the door. "Leo has been hacking every camera he can between the hospital and the clinic and working out from there to try to catch sight of the ambushers. It was three vamps and a half dozen blighthounds. Poor medics didn't have a chance. But they vanished into the forest again pretty quickly and Leo can't find them on any more cameras. That road may be a freeway, but it's not exactly a busy one."

Aldric dragged himself out of the truck and into the house. The place was strangely quiet for the number of people he could sense in the building. That sixth sense that everyone has for when a space is empty or not almost vibrated with the presence of so many people.

"I want to check in with Faith, then I will come to your office. Coffee would be very welcome." Aldric needed to see her. To hold her for just a minute and reassure himself that she was safe. Then he could face the next steps in this mess.

Marc nodded. "I think she's sulking in her room. She didn't like that I wouldn't let her head right to the clinic. Two of our sentries as bodyguards and two cops should be enough to get Lincoln to the city safely enough. You said they snuck him out?"

"Yes. They are heading in a civilian van, and Lincoln was stretched out across several seats. I sent two of our best, and Steven was one of the police officers riding along," Aldric answered as he headed for the stairs. It was good to know that even one of the humans in the van knew the truth of the matter. Steven was married into the clan, after all. "Oh, Maria is expecting their first pup. I warned him not to get injured or she would kill him."

Marc snorted. "At least there is some good news coming out of this summer. I'll get your coffee then give her a call." Marc waved him off and headed towards the kitchen, and Aldric turned with a relieved sigh to the stairs.

They were daunting, he was so tired.

It was more of an exhaustion of the spirit than of the body. He had been woken early, yes, but he had gotten adequate sleep and had only been up for six hours. Aunt Lucy frowned at him when he reached the top of the stairs.

"You look terrible," she said.

"I have been up for some time now," he answered simply.

She nodded and walked beside him down the hall. "I heard. How is the detective?"

"He is in poor shape but he will heal. I am rather glad that he has let his dislike of me show only in his words, however. I do not think I would enjoy being roasted." He had to admit, Detective Lincoln was a warrior at heart, and a skilled one. Aldric was not at all certain that he could win a full-on battle with the man.

"I'm glad to hear it. Both that he will heal and that you don't want to get set ablaze. Faith will be quite relieved as well. I understand that she was furious that Marc wouldn't let her go to you." She looked at him with a serious expression. "I have been learning a lot about you over the short time I have been here. I agree with Faith's assessment. You are a good man. More importantly to an old woman, you are good to my girl. She may have been born to my brother and sister-in-law, but she and Crissy are the daughters of my heart. I haven't much cared for the men she has dated in the past, and I think it may be a stretch to call what you have been doing *dating*, but nevertheless. You have my blessing."

Aldric stopped just outside Faith's door and stared at Lucy, shocked.

Lucy chuckled. "Yes, yes. I know. But consider it parental approval. I think they would have like you."

"Thank you." He didn't know what else to say. Lucy just smiled and patted his shoulder.

"Now, that niece of mine has been sulking all morning. Didn't even come to have breakfast. You get in there and drag her back into the action, you hear? At least into the planning. I'll go play with the kids and see what else I can do to help. If I can organize a production meeting and herd actors and models through a dozen soundstages, I'm sure I can help plan a war." Lucy winked at him, then turned and walked away.

Aldric felt like she simply told the truth. He almost felt some pity for the poor vampires who held Crissy. Almost.

He knocked at Faith's door. "Faith? May I come in?"

There was no answer, and he wondered if perhaps she had fallen asleep.

"Faith?" he knocked again and listened carefully. The room sounded empty. He turned the knob and pushed the door open to confirm his suspicion.

With a frown, he pulled the door closed and went searching. She was not in his room or the den or the room they called the library. His frown deepened as he began systematically searching the entire clan house, from top to bottom. Faith was nowhere to be found.

Aldric stalked into Marc's office.

Marc's smirk froze half-formed when he saw Aldric's expression. "Where have you been then? I assumed…"

"She is not here."

"I have been searching the house. I wished to do a discreet search here before I started alarming anyone." Aldric knew he sounded calm, his voice steady and even, but inside his mind, he was screaming. The last time he felt this sort of panic was when Kaylee and Jake had been taken, but even that fear had not been this sharp.

Marc seemed to understand that. He simply reached for his phone. "Tamika? Hey, could you do me a favor and check the security footage around the house? Yes. Since this morning. Um," Marc narrowed his eyes, thinking. "Last I saw her was just after seven. So seven A.M. till now. Yes. Anything you find."

Marc simply nodded and hung up after that. "She's going to check. You are going to sit down and drink this coffee, then the blood pack I'm going to bring you. If anything has happened we're going to need you at full strength."

Aldric bit back a snarl and nodded. Lashing out at Marc would do no good. How could someone have gotten into the clan house undetected? They had not taken Kaylee as well, Aldric had seen her in the den with Jake and Lucy and a handful of sentries who all seemed to be enjoying a movie marathon. Any other time and he would have been amused by how invested the adults seemed to be in the animated film.

He had passed Greg Honeyford on his way back out of that wing as well. The teacher had been carrying a few bags that seemed to be full of craft supplies to set up in the room that Marc had designated the classroom. When asked, Greg had not seen Faith but had heard about the attack and asked after the detective.

Tamika in his office had not seen her either, nor had Frankie at the front door, or Uncle Eldridge in the kitchen who seemed to be there to see Lucy. Aldric did not wish to think too hard about how his uncle had come to be in the clan house when the lockdown order had come through. Eldridge was not the sort to disobey an order of that sort.

"Here." Marc's hand on his shoulder stopped his pacing and brought him back to the present. A mug was shoved into his hands, a blood pack warming in the water.

"Tamika's on her way in. She says she found something," Marc said. "She also said she wanted to be here when we see it."

Aldric did snarl at that, but he sat with his blood and drank. Marc was right about that much at least. He would need his energy.

"Here's the bit you want to see." Tamika was talking before she even entered the room. She carried her laptop and set it on the edge of the desk so that all three of them could watch, then tapped a button and the timestamp started playing.

The image was from the camera in the garage. It was situated over the door, to show who was leaving or entering in a vehicle, and showed a fair portion of the interior while another was positioned to show the interior door.

They watched as, at 7:08 a.m. Frankie jogged into the frame, carrying a travel mug and speaking on the phone. Whoever he was speaking to seemed to be doing most of the talking. He went straight to one of the security SUVs and unlocked it, and reached inside for a moment, then turned back to lean casually on the door frame be the driver's seat.

A moment later he hung up and tapped something into his phone. He was peering at his screen when his attention jerked up to the interior door a second before Faith rushed up to him. He grinned and shrugged when she said something and handed her the travel mug, and her eyes got huge before she gave him a quick hug and took a long sip.

Frankie laughed and gestured, then turned to the car. Faith scurried around to the passenger side and got in, and was taking another sip as Frankie drove the vehicle out of the shot. By 7:11 a.m. Faith and Frankie were headed away from the clan house.

Aldric's vision had hazed and he knew he was presenting as fully vampire.

"I'll get Frankie," Tamika said. "You take a few moments and get yourself together. We need you, Aldric, and we need you not feral."

Tamika using his name instead of calling him *sugar* brought him up short and he realized that he had been growling for several minutes. He took the opportunity she presented and breathed deep. Marc watched him carefully but didn't speak. Aldric pulled his temper back with what was likely a visible effort.

Marc just nodded then flicked his eyes up as Tamika returned with Frankie in tow.

"We just need to clear something up, and we know you've been here all morning," Tamika was saying as she led the sentry into the office.

Aldric managed to nod politely, at the man when he came in, all bright and helpful. "Sure thing, whatever I can help with."

Frankie's smile was wide, but there was always the sadness of recent loss in his eyes now. Aldric was not inclined to feel sympathetic just at the moment, no matter how much he missed Mia as well.

"Frankie, thanks for your help," Marc said.

Aldric kept silent, sure that if he opened his mouth he would hiss and threaten rather than use words. They didn't know for certain that Frankie had done anything wrong.

No, he corrected himself. *We know he left the house, with Faith, after the lockdown order went out.* That at least was enough to have this conversation with the man.

Frankie had been making some poor choices the past few weeks. It was understandable, given the strange ways grief works, which is the only reason that Marc and the rest of the inner circle hadn't come down on him harder already. They had each taken the man aside to talk and to let him know that they were there for him if he needed them.

It was clear that had not been enough.

"So, we have this video here that we're hoping you can give us some insight into," Tamika was saying. "We'd love to know everything you can tell us about it."

"Sure, whatever I can do to help," Frankie answered.

His voice sounded tighter to Aldric, as if he had any

idea what was coming. Good. He should be aware that he made a serious error in judgment, and would be subjected to serious punishment for it.

When the video finished, Frankie shrugged. "She said she wanted to go to the clinic. I offered her a ride."

Marc leaned forward over his desk, and Aldric felt the touch of his friend's authority. "You knew there was a lockdown for security reasons, Frankie. You knew perfectly clearly that nobody was supposed to be going anywhere."

"Sure," Frankie said. "But we'll be much safer now, without the vamps coming after her the Goldfangs won't have any backup. Everything will be back to normal in a few days."

There was dead silence in the office as Frankie stood there, an odd but satisfied smile on his face. The moment passed as Aldric's furious scream rattled the house and Frankie found himself pinned to the far wall of the office by Aldric's hand around his throat.

CHAPTER 11

Aldric could hear Marc and Tamika shouting, and more voices from the door, but the anger and the grief and the betrayal were screaming in his ears and the only sounds that he could hear with any clarity were the terrified whimpers coming from the worm he had pinned.

"Where is she?" He hissed the words, his vampiric nature fully in command and his words sounding more like a snake's hissing around his fangs. Nevertheless, he would find her and he would destroy anyone that stood in his way, starting with this wolf. "What did you do to her? Where is my mate?"

Frankie whimpered and Aldric could smell fear and a touch of ammonia as the dead wolf pissed himself.

"Aldric." A strong hand landed on his shoulder and tugged him hard enough to shift his attention slightly. Uncle Eldridge stood there, his gentle features twisted by fangs and blood-dark eyes. He was ready to face his nephew if necessary and that fact was what pulled Aldric back from the blind, focused rage that rode him.

"Aldric, Frankie can't answer if he can't breathe,"

Eldridge said. "And your shouting has frightened the children. And several others in the house."

None of them had needed to draw on the full depth of their predatory natures since they fought in World War Two; the first time vampires actively hunted mages. Very few of those who were in the clan house at the moment had ever seen a vampire in his full strength. Only those who had been at the lodge when Aldric had torn his way through dozens of bodies to get to Faith and the children.

Aldric couldn't answer without hissing, so he simply nodded, and lowered Frankie to his feet. He did not release his grip, though he loosened it enough to allow the wolf to breathe. And speak.

"Holy shit," Tamika said softly.

"I knew you were holding back some, Aldric, but damn." Marc whistled. "Tamika, go let everyone know we're safe and the situation is handled. We'll pick this up again in a minute."

"I remember the way your father looked at your mother when they met, you know," Eldridge was speaking to him in a low voice. "And I've seen how you look at Faith when you think nobody is watching. I know, Aldric. I know a little of what you're feeling, but you need to stay calm. Faith needs you to stay calm. You can't help her if you are letting your rage direct your actions. We need answers right now more than we need vengeance."

Aldric snarled but nodded.

"Okay. I have him. He isn't going anywhere. You can step back now," Eldridge said. "Marc has Frankie's other arm. There's no way he's going anywhere from here but the interrogation room. Okay?"

Marc's soft rumble of agreement made Aldric blink. He hadn't even been aware of his friend coming close. He nodded and released his hold on Frankie, then sped to the other side of the room. Eldridge was right. Blind fury had never, in the long history of life on Earth, solved any problem. He needed information from the ex-sentry, and to get it, he needed to find enough calm to speak. To actually be able to hear the answers.

Aldric stared out the window into the backyard, seeing not what lay in front of him, but a movie strip of memories of Faith being introduced to the Frostwalkers, of her chatting and laughing with her new clanmates. Of her playing with Kaylee and Jake and defending them during the surprise attack, and smiling at him as they walked in the evening and talked about everything they could think of, important or not.

Aldric would find her. There was no acceptable alternative.

"I've called Kenya and Ori back here, and sent a trio of sentries to take over at the cabin so Rod can come as well," Marc's voice broke into his thoughts. "We're going to have all hands on deck within the hour. Leo and his friend are hacking every traffic camera, private security camera, and ATM cam they can to track the route Frankie took. They've already traced him as far as the freeway onramp, but there aren't a ton of cameras on the freeway after that, we're too far from the city, so when you're ready we can go interrogate Frankie."

Marc huffed out a heavy sigh and ran his fingers through his hair. "We're out of holding cells. We never had this many near-rogues to worry about and holding enemies from a pack war was never what that space was meant for."

Aldric dug deep. "Those rogues that were with Honeyford at the beginning have become much less feral thanks to your frequent visits to the cells, and several have indicated an interest in finding a true pack. Perhaps those individuals can be moved to a less secure location."

His voice still had the sibilance of his vampiric anger, but the words were clear.

"You are very right, Aldric. Perhaps we can shuffle things around a bit. Matthias is already integrating into our clan, a bit. He asked if he could take over meal prep while I was so busy, and he's been a huge help." Marc chuckled. "The first time I thanked him for it, he about fainted. I don't think he is used to being appreciated."

"It is good to know that not all of the Goldfang wolves are irredeemable." Aldric concentrated and his vision shifted a bit more toward his human self.

"True enough." Marc nodded. "Hell, not even all Honeyfords are that bad. Greg's a sweetheart and damned clever. You should see what he's doing in the schoolroom I offered to him."

"Kaylee gets another guard," Aldric said. "And Lucy gets one as well."

"Already done," Marc said. "And I checked in on them to let Lucy know what was happening and see that the kids were okay after your, uh..."

"Indeed," Aldric was not ashamed of his reaction to learning of Frankie's betrayal, but he did regret that he may have frightened the children.

"They're fine. I explained that you were very angry, but not at them. They seemed to understand that, but you might drop in to say hello in a little bit. When you've completely pulled yourself together."

Aldric nodded. "I did not intend to frighten them."

"Nobody thinks you did." His uncle smiled at him, a small, encouraging expression. "You can check in with them later. Right now we have a wolf to talk to."

They all trooped to the basement holding area and Aldric took a few deep breaths before he opened the door to the room they were using as an interrogation room.

Kenya and Ori were already there, and the playful expressions they usually wore were nowhere in evidence.

Frankie sat at the table, glaring at the pair. His chin was up and his shoulders were back, but in his lap, his fingers shook and he squeezed them so tight that his knuckles turned white. He wore sweatpants now, and Aldric wondered vaguely who had thought of that.

Wordlessly he stepped into the room, followed by Marc. Uncle Eldridge stayed upstairs in the kitchen to help soothe anyone still nervous after Aldric's surge of temper. He still wasn't calm, but he could pretend he was until they had the information they needed.

"Frankie," Marc said in the same tone a disappointed father would after being called to a meeting with the principal. "Frankie, tell us what happened."

Frankie glared around the room until his eyes landed on Aldric, and he sneered.

"All our problems started when that woman came here. That was when the Goldfangs attacked. That was when the vamps showed up. That was when you all decided to help some random stranger. And for what? She's just a human. There's millions of them out there." Frankie snorted. "It doesn't make any damn sense why everyone wants one boring-looking human woman, but whatever. They want her, they can have her. We're all safer now."

Aldric blinked at the venom in the man's voice. Marc seemed surprised by it as well and frowned.

"You do understand that wasn't your choice to make," he said. His voice and posture were relaxed and calm, but Aldric had known him long enough to hear the anger in his tone. "The Frostwalker Clan is dedicated to helping others. To serving our community as a whole, not to pick and choose who *deserves* our help. The Lathams were attacked by rogues in their own home, inside our territory.

That alone is reason enough to give them shelter and protection."

"But that doesn't explain why those vampires want her." Frankie leaned forward. "And besides that, if you'd just sent them to the cops like you should have, none of this would have happened! My sweet Mia would still be here." With the last sentence, his voice broke and his whole body shook.

And it all came together for Aldric. Mia was the enforcer that had been killed in the first rescue attempt at the lodge. They had gone after Crissy and the children at the location Jessie Honeyford was holding them in an old rustic corporate retreat, and they had succeeded in rescuing the three from the semi-rogue wolves.

Nobody had counted on being immediately ambushed by vampires driving nearly a full pack of blighthounds. They had snatched Crissy and very nearly taken Faith and the children as well, but for her magic shield. Mia had died in the second wave attack.

"Frankie," Marc sighed. He rubbed his fingers over his forehead and seemed almost like he bowed as he shouldered the weight of this revelation. "We knew that you were grieving. We all are. But—"

"He's not!" Frankie pointed an accusing finger at Aldric and it took every ounce of self-control for him not to react. Frankie's bravado faded in the face of Aldric's stony, unmoving expression, but he forged on anyway, even as he hunched in on himself. "Aldric's not grieving, he doesn't give a damn! All he cares about is fucking that—"

Aldric didn't have to move. Ori did it for him, getting right into Frankie's face and snarling, the sound much more wolf than man. "I would not finish that sentence if I were you. You claim to have loved Mia? You want to convince us that you were even worthy to even speak to her? You start behaving like it. Mia would never have looked twice at you if she'd known what you were capable of," he growled out, the words raspy and thick as his tongue tried forming them around teeth too sharp to make it easy for human speech.

"Mia loved knowing that she was strong enough to protect those who needed it, and anyone that needed her help was welcome to it. All of us are Enforcers for that reason. Not to pick and choose who is *worthy,* and certainly not to judge who our leaders fall in love with. You say you loved her? Bullshit. You're just another ego-filled asshole who views his partners as possessions. You're not even worthy to speak her name."

Ori spat the last words like they were bullets before retreating to the wall beside Kenya again, growling the whole time while Frankie cringed and whimpered in his chair.

Marc cleared his throat. He glanced over at Aldric who was seething but kept himself from even twitching. This was a man they had all considered offering an Enforcer spot to? How had they not seen this side of the man?

"So." Marc dragged the word out a little, visibly organizing his next words. "Tell us about this morning. Who did you call in the garage?"

Frankie glared at Ori, then at Marc, like a sullen child. "One of the mercenaries the Goldfangs picked up. I knew him a bit a few years back, and he doesn't care. It's just a job to him." Frankie shrugged. "He said to call him if I ever heard something that'd help. He pointed out that getting rid of *her* would solve more than half our problems."

Aldric did growl now, and he wasn't alone. Frankie paled further and sent him a wary glance, but the petulant tone of voice didn't change at all.

"She *wanted* to go out, against your orders, Alpha," Frankie whined as if that statement would help him out of the enormous hole he'd dug for himself. "So I called my old buddy and told him that we were heading out and that I'd drive real slow and carefully. I already had some sleeping pills since Mia died, so I put them in her coffee and when my buddy showed up down the street, she was asleep. Nobody else needs to get hurt!"

"So you arranged for a mercenary, who is working for the Goldfang Stalkers, to know the position and movements of the very person we have been trying to keep out of their hands *at all costs*, thus not only rendering our precautions useless but also making Mia's death mean nothing at all. She died for *nothing*." Aldric couldn't keep silent any longer. "And now you may have fueled the spark kindling another World War."

Frankie jumped his seat and all the rest of the blood drained from his face.

"I–"

"This is what revenge does, Frankie," Marc said, shaking his head and sounding every bit like the disappointed father again. "It blinds us. It weakens us. It makes us vulnerable to manipulation. That's what happened here, do you realize that? Your so-called *buddy* saw that you were a weak point in our defense, and he exploited you."

Marc sighed and leaned back in his chair.

"I think it's long past time to answer Aldric's earlier question. Where is Faith now?"

Frankie slumped and his sulky huff would have done any teenager proud. "I don't know. Why the hell should I know?"

CHATPER 12

I t was cold and her arms felt like lead, so reaching for the blanket was more work than she wanted to do. Why it was so cold Faith had no idea, but there was a faint breeze, too. It seemed like someone had cranked up the air conditioning and then left the window open.

Or... something niggled in the back of her mind. Something she should remember. Something important. Maybe it was related to why it smelled a bit like stale socks and dried blood? Or... they did wash the clothes from when they had fallen into that cave, hadn't they? That's what it smelled like. They had gotten out of there, hadn't they? This wasn't some sort of weird situation where she had only dreamed that she fed Aldric and then they escaped the cave and rescued Greg Honeyford and Aunt Lucy knew about magic?

That would make a weird amount of sense, though. And it would explain why her head felt so *foggy*. And when she tried to pull on her magic, to throw up a shield, pull up a fireball, anything, the magic was just as fuzzy as her thoughts. It was like trying to hold water in her hand- it kept leaking away, back into the ether or wherever it lived.

"Oh, come now, I heard your breathing change five minutes ago. I know you're awake." A voice intruded into her musings. It was warm like melted honey and the words were accented in an almost sexy sort of way, but she couldn't quite place it. The voice may have been pleasant, but the tone was definitely not. "Time to open your eyes."

Faith didn't follow directions, and instead did a mental scan of herself. Her body felt weak, a little like when she surfaced to almost wake up in the middle of the night but didn't quite make it all the way awake. Thinking was a little tough as her mind did not want to stay focused, and odd, random thoughts kept popping into her brain. Overall she felt sluggish and fuzzy. What the hell *happened?*

She must have said that last thought out loud because the rude man with the nice voice answered.

"You were brought to me at last, Magaestra, that is what happened," The voice crowed. There was a huff of irritation almost immediately after. "How I managed to fall in with such useless fools as those wolves, I still do not know. I am not accustomed to such repeated failure."

Oh shit.

Faith forced her eyes open and checked her body again. Did it feel like she had been bitten anywhere? When Aldric bit her the wound itself closed up quickly, but there was a tingle in her arm for several hours, even after there was no longer any visible evidence of the bite.

No tingles now, just the finally fading heaviness.

"I have been told that the drug will be fully out of your system within the next twelve hours. I look forward to breakfast." A man in an expensive suit leered at her from a sumptuous armchair. Dark blond hair framed dark eyes and a tanned complexion. He would probably have been handsome if he wasn't so clearly an arrogant, kidnapping asshole, Faith thought vaguely.

Even in her fuzzy brain, she thought it looked a bit much when combined with his suit— three-piece and distinctly high-end— and the rug underneath his feet— cream-colored and plush with some faint geometric pattern all over, from what she could see of it. Faith blinked and looked around to see a low, white table with scrolled legs and nothing on it, another chair to match the one Rich Guy sat in was white as well, with the wood details painted gold and a perfectly plumped, bright, fire-engine red pillow resting in the seat.

She didn't want to think of the name that hovered around the edge of her mind. That would make it too real.

Curtains were draping the entire wall behind the man, cream again with a tasteful pattern of red stripes to match the pillow. The curtains ended high above their heads and seemed to stretch up and up only to disappear into darkness near the ceiling. Or at least she couldn't tell what was above them, as the light from the lamps near them almost glowed off the fabric of the carpet and the furniture. Everything she *could* see screamed expensive, luxurious, and egotistical. It was a movie set for a rich man that wanted to pretend he lived at his country club.

Faith rolled her head, but all she could see was the back of the sofa she was laying on. White, again, with a fuzzy red blanket thrown tastefully over the back. The fabric under her cheek felt like velvet.

"Well?" the man demanded. "Sit up. I have been waiting."

Faith groaned. "Screw you. I don't follow your orders, buddy, I'm not one of your low-rent thugs."

Given the surroundings that she could make out, Faith made a reasonable guess that his ego would be more than a little vulnerable. She smirked when he growled at her in response.

"It is extremely unwise to anger me," he said. "I am Sandalio Conti and you are nothing."

Faith struggled to sit up. She was feeling better by the minute, though she wouldn't want to run any marathons for a while. Stall. She had to stall until Aldric found her. She was one hundred percent sure that Aldric *would* find her, too. She just had to be patient. And stall.

"I am important enough to stick around and send out shitty mercenaries and the Goldfang idiots," Faith smirked. "And you didn't answer my question. Although I doubt I'd believe you whatever you said."

Conti scowled. "I can make your life comfortable or very, very unpleasant."

"You've already made it unpleasant," Faith shot back. "Have been for weeks, so why change things up now?"

Conti's scowl slid into a more excited expression. Faith wasn't sure it could qualify as a smile though he likely would call it such. It was cold and joyless but still gleeful at the same time. Her immediate reaction was to try to pull at her magic, but it remained out of her reach. *Think!* she commanded herself. *Ken talked about this! About how it's hard to focus sometimes. God, why did I have to turn it into a joke about coffee? What did he say?*

"Let me assure you that I have not even tried to make your life unpleasant. Yet." Conti settled back in his chair and reached for a glass on the small table beside him.

"Did you escape from a bad movie? Are you seriously drinking blood out of a wine glass?" Faith couldn't stop the words. She needed to get better control of her mouth in situations like this.

Conti ignored her and sipped at his drink.

Faith took the opportunity to look around herself.

What had seemed like a large, ornate room when she first woke was in reality far bigger than she had thought. In fact, it seemed that the ceiling wasn't the fancy drywall or plaster high-ceiling that she had expected, but stretched away into the dusty shadows that looked industrial. She could just make out steel girders some ways above the draped fabrics that covered the walls.

Faith glanced at the fabric and realized that they didn't simply cover the walls, they essentially *were* the walls. The opening at one corner stretched all the way to the top of the drapery and was the same quality dusty dimness as the space above them. She was in some sort of huge, open space that was divided up by fancy drapery and expensive furnishings.

"Where's Crissy?" At least she could get some information, maybe.

"Who?" Conti's brow twitched as if his instinct was to frown but he couldn't bear to lower himself to that crass level of expression.

"My sister," Faith growled. "Where is my sister Crissy?"

"Ahh, the mage that the Goldfangs thought they could keep. She is here," he waved vaguely at one of the curtained walls. "She tried to put up a bit of fight, not that she was any real challenge for my people. An untrained mage throwing a punch at a vampire?" A smile flickered across his lips. "It was amusing. But she has been much less of a nuisance since she has been here."

"What have you done to her?" Faith was determined to reach her magic and hold on to it. Keep him talking. She snickered to herself a bit, remembering a snatch dialogue from the villain of Jake's favorite movie. *Got to get him monologuing.*

"Oh, nothing too detrimental. For the moment, at least. She is a valuable resource, after all, and one must take care of one's livestock. We are storing her blood away to be gifted to those of my people who prove themselves worthy," Conti smiled indulgently. "She tastes lovely, even though her magic is weak. I have enjoyed learning about my new abilities, however."

He flicked the fingers of his free hand and a shower of sparks arced out in front of him, dancing through the air like fireflies. "A fire mage. Not a powerful one, as I said, so I will require several more meals from her, but it doesn't take much fire to blind someone."

It took all of Faith's willpower not to growl and launch herself at him. She didn't need magic to blind this jackass. Tamika had shown her a few tricks that she didn't even need claws for.

"You see, the one aspect of my mentor's operations that I truly disagree with was the wastefulness that was encouraged." Conti waved his hand and the sparks danced into a waving net between them, then flowed into a swirl around him.

"All those mages drained on-site by whoever caught them, or brought to him and Master Wilhelm to be drained by them. Such careless squandering of valuable resources! Then the vampires who took the blood, who gained that power? They were untrained, unfocused, and often sloppy, getting killed quickly and uselessly. My forces will be much more carefully organized, with the blood magic being granted to those who prove their worth. Once I have enough blood stored from you two, and that detective fellow, I will start selecting my elite soldiers. My special forces, if you will. I can't wait to be able to rely on actual warriors instead of those worthless wolves and their weak, gullible Alpha."

Faith clamped her teeth together, willing herself not to throw up. Holy shit, this guy *actually was* planning to start

World War Three! Uncle Eldridge had tossed it out as possible after Leo found that photo of Conti and the other guy, but nobody had seriously thought that was possible. A soft growl from somewhere nearby snapped her out of her panic spiral, but Conti didn't seem to hear it.

Come on, what was it that Ken had said to do when the magic felt so slippery? If she got out of this she was going to apologize to him and start doing the meditation as he suggested.

"You, however?" Conti peered at her like she was a curious animal at a zoo. "You have some very interesting abilities if the reports are true. Tell me, how did you keep yourself and those children protected when we acquired your sister?"

Faith growled now. Tamika would be proud of the sound Faith managed. "Fuck you."

Conti chuckled. "I don't often lower myself to associate with *humans* like that." He put his glass down and leaned forward. "Tell me."

"No."

Conti sat back in his chair, an amused smirk spreading across his face.

"It doesn't matter terribly, I suppose," he said, his accent softening his words, making them sound less violent and the incongruence was terrifying. "I shall find out soon enough. Until then, I shall simply reinforce my current skills before I gain new ones."

He waved the sparks back into the space between them and reached for his glass again.

He sipped slowly and smiled and Faith bit her cheek to prevent herself from screaming.

CHAPTER 13

I t had been hours. *Hours* since they discovered Faith's kidnapping. Frankie had admitted that he drugged the coffee he gave her in the car with two crushed-up pills Madeline had prescribed him after Mia's death and that she had gone under relatively quickly. A quick call to Madeline had confirmed that Faith was likely in no medical danger from it, though the fact that she succumbed so quickly concerned Madeline.

It didn't surprise Aldric, however. Faith had once explained that drugs, even prescribed ones, made her nervous after watching a friend of hers get addicted to painkillers in high school. She herself rarely took anything stronger than over-the-counter pain medicine, even when she should. Madeline assured him that was likely a factor, as well as the fact that Faith hadn't eaten breakfast before leaving, so the drug passed quickly into her system.

None of that was reassuring to Aldric, however, since Faith wasn't *here* for Madeline to examine. *She should be fine* was not a useful sentiment when *fine* also included not being held by psychotic vampires bent on some sort of movie villain world domination scheme. Faith was *not fine* and Aldric was pacing the clan house like a caged tiger, waiting for *someone* to come up with any useful damn information.

"That's enough of that." Lucy grabbed his wrist as he stalked down the hallway, and tugged him in the other direction. "You are making everyone nervous and you've frightened the children to the point that Greg took them to the half-finished schoolroom to get them involved in a project. Jake shifted twice when you stomped past the den."

Aldric blinked at the back of Lucy's head as she pulled him along.

"I know that you're anxious about Faith and furious at that traitorous asshole, but that is no reason to take it out on the rest of us. We're all worried and angry," Lucy said. She stopped at the kitchen table and tugged until she had him seated, then pinned him there with a glare. "You park your butt right there, Aldric Donnelly and you find some damn calm. I'll make tea."

"I did not intend to frighten the children," he said. He couldn't keep the slight hiss from his voice, letting anyone who listened know that he was stomping furiously around the house *with fangs* even if his face remained human.

Lucy raised an eyebrow but remained silent and turned back to pour the hot water into mugs. Teabags went into the water and she bustled everything away quickly before bringing the mugs to the table.

"Chamomile. You could use a little soothing." She set the steaming drink in front of him and he could smell the sweet, bitter herbs. It had never been his favorite tea, but he was not going to turn down any help in settling the fury he was feeling. Lucy was correct in that he should not be unsettling the others in the house.

He *should* be doing something productive to find Faith.

While Aldric couldn't concentrate on anything other than imagining the bloody end of Cherro and his minions, Marc and Tamika were glued to their phones and their computers, trying to track down where Frankie took his Faith– And that was it wasn't it? As he frowned at the tea, Aldric realized that it was far from the first time that he had thought of Faith as *his* in some way.

He breathed deeply over the steam and sipped his team, to an approving nod from Lucy.

"I hear that you did not react very calmly when Frankie's actions came to light?" Lucy said. Her voice was mild and her words were casual, but the look in her eye was shrewd. "I *hear* that you referred to my niece as your mate?"

Aldric choked on his sip of tea, liquid dribbling down his chin as he coughed. He grabbed a nearby napkin and dabbed at himself before looking up at Lucy, wide-eyed. The look in her eye was now amused more than anything, but her expression was otherwise unchanged.

"Mmmm, I thought you might have done that in the heat of the moment, but you know. Often that *is* when our subconscious brain can get through to us," she said. Then she smiled, just a small flicker of pleasure. "Does she know how you feel?"

Aldric blinked at the small human woman.

"I..."

Lucy laughed and reached over to pat his arm. "You tell her when you see her."

"Assuming we can find her in time. I may never let her out of my sight again," Aldric admitted, and Lucy laughed again.

"Eldridge told me a little bit about bonding," she said. "You're well on your way, aren't you? You should tell her that, as well."

Aldric froze, his mind reeling from the shock of having his world suddenly slot into a sensible, understandable pattern. How did... *When* did...

"Oh, sweetie. You've been going full tilt at this problem and haven't slowed down enough to even think about anything else, have you?" Lucy patted his arm again and then wrapped both hands around her mug.

"I admit that when I got here I was... concerned. That Crissy was missing, and that Faith had found refuge among the very sort of people that she was supposed to avoid, according to my sister-in-law. But It didn't take me very long to see how everyone around here adores Kaylee, or how protective you all are of both of them. They're family now. That at least, is clear as a summer day. But you?" She cocked an eyebrow at him and smirked over her mug. "You always know where they are, both of them, and if you don't, you get anxious and seek them out. You are well past *attached* and headed straight for *stupid with it* in the most adorable way. Except for right now with all the hissing and the scary aura wafting off you."

Aldric frowned, thinking. Lucy was right. Since the day he had brought Faith and Kaylee here, he always made sure to know where they were and who they were with. The few times he didn't *know*, everything had gone distinctly wrong. Kaylee and Jake had been snatched off the street. Faith and Kaylee had been attacked in the back-yard while Detective Lincoln stood there. And today, while he was at the clinic and certain that Faith was safe, asleep in her bed in a house full of security, she was being drugged and whisked right out from under their very noses.

And he was falling apart.

With a deep sigh, he looked up at Lucy. "What do I do? What do I do if..."

Lucy pursed her lips. "Well, first. Don't think that way. If you assume the worst, that is what you will get. Funny thing about the universe: it tends to be more than happy to fulfill your expectations."

Aldric grimaced.

"Second, you find your Zen or whatever and get to work. Marc and Tamika have been calling all over getting in touch with people that could maybe have information for them, and I don't mean just Frostwalker people either. Humans, the odd stray, other packs, and covens. Whoever they can get in touch with that might know something. And Leo is damned close to growing a USB port in the side of his head or some such. He hasn't left his computer chair since we found out."

Lucy raised her brows at him and nodded at his tepid tea. "Finish your tea and get to work. You'll feel more settled when you have a task in front of you."

Aldric nodded and did as he was told. Lucy smiled and patted his shoulder when she stood up to go rinse her mug.

"Good boy. I like you for her, you know. You bring out her real smile." Lucy clucked her tongue and rolled her eyes. "A significant improvement over her last date. I can't even dignify that jerk with the title *boyfriend*."

"Thank you?" Aldric finished his tea, even though it was cold, and handed it to the small woman when she held her hand out for it.

"Now, off you go. Marc is probably ready to update you on what they've been doing." Lucy turned back to the sink dismissing him.

Aldric blinked. His vision doubled for just a moment, seeing a different woman standing there, washing a different dish, but having just as easily set him straight. He didn't know if reincarnation was a thing or not, but if it was, then he would not be shocked to learn that Lucy's soul had once resided in the Frostwalker's last Magaestra.

Shaking his head, he turned and headed for Marc's office.

Marc glanced up warily when Aldric entered, and Aldric ducked his head.

"I apologize. I... I have not been handling my anxiety well," Aldric said. It was an understatement, but he couldn't think of better words to use.

Marc relaxed visibly and nodded. "I understand, Aldric. I wasn't much less crazy when Jake was taken if I recall."

It was true enough. Marc had been half-shifted at one point, ready to tear apart anyone that stood between him and his son.

"Have we learned anything?"

Marc growled. "Nothing that we didn't already know. We've been looking for these guys for weeks, and still nothing," Marc grimaced. "Leo lost the SUV on the freeway—the same freeway that the ambulance was ambushed on, though, so at least it's a clue."

He waved Aldric over and showed him a map on his computer screen that had overlapping circles drawn on it. Marc pointed at each in turn.

"Okay, so this one's centered on us, here. We figured that it wouldn't make much sense to come hauling in from too far away, and from here to the Goldfang's camp was not a terrible guess as far as distance, we decided. So these circles have a radius of five miles. Either a wolf or a vampire could easily travel that distance for an attack, and it wouldn't be much more than that to drive on the roads rather than in a straight line like they could on foot."

Aldric nodded. Five miles was nothing. Even a human

could travel that distance relatively easily, though it would take them longer. "And the other circles?"

Marc moved his finger to point. "This is centered on the Goldfang's camp. This one is the Latham's cabin. This is where the ambulance was attacked. These two green ones are known entrances to that mine cave system. We're not sure if that is useful or relevant information, but Leo and I decided to put it up there anyway. He's been checking for increased activity in both of those locations, but nothing so far."

"Has Tamika found anything?"

Marc shook his head. "Not that she's said, and if she had, she would have come running in to tell me. She's been calling sentries and running down Frankie's whole life trying to figure out who this 'old buddy' is and where they are now. Frankie has clammed up. Once he understood that we didn't agree that he had done us any favors by removing Faith from the house, he completely shut down."

He sighed heavily and his shoulders slumped. "I should have seen how destroyed he was. How badly the grief shook him up. I knew that he was a mess for days after Mia died, and he could barely stand through the ceremony in the memorial grove, but..." Marc grimaced again.

Aldric put a hand on his friend's shoulder and squeezed lightly. "As you said, grief affects us all differently. As I myself displayed this morning." Aldric's smile was rueful. "I did not mean to frighten everyone in the house."

"Well, I hear we are going to get some fantastic art project out of it from the kids. Greg is a godsend and the complete opposite of his brother. How those two are related, I'll never understand." Marc shook his head slowly. "I suppose you can't pick your family."

"You can't pick your genetics," Aldric said. "Family, I think, is what you make of it."

CHATPER 14

Faith shivered in the cold of the room. It must have been at least an hour since she woke up here, and lord only knows how long she was asleep in the first place. There were no windows that she could see, and no clocks in this little fancy pop-up room to tell her how long she had been here. Her stomach was growling every so often and she was pretty sure that Conti heard it, but he gave no indication that he cared.

Her friends had to have realized she was missing by now. Aldric would have tried to find her when he got home, even if he was just going to go right to bed. He had gotten into the habit of checking in with her when he came in from his patrols, and any other time he headed out. She had thought of it as a sweet habit, but now it might save her life.

Assuming they could track her down.

"If I starve to death it won't help you much, will it?" she said after a particularly loud protest from her stomach. She should have eaten something for breakfast before she let Frankie kidnap her.

She hoped that Aldric and the rest had figured out that Frankie was a traitorous asshole already.

"That is true. But you slept through the human feeding for the day." Conti shrugged. "Although I suppose that is a bit of a generous statement as it is only you and the one other at the moment. Still, those Goldfangs in the kitchen have more important people to worry about feeding than you."

Oh, she couldn't wait to punch this guy in the face. Or straight through the ribcage with an invisible spike.

"Now listen here, you pathetic excuse for a b-movie villain–"

"Sandy!" a new voice rang out, interrupting her snarling protest. "Sandy, have you had lunch yet? I think it is lunchtime."

The man that hurried into the light now was thin, but still handsome. Dark hair with a hint of a wave in it fell boyishly over his forehead and soft brown eyes almost sparkled with his good mood. Unlike the creepy, slightly crazy smile Conti occasionally flashed at her, the newcomer wore a charming smile and aimed it at Faith. Reyher Cherro was much more handsome than in the photo Leo had found.

Faith was in a lot of trouble.

"Oh, and who is our guest? You should have told me we had a visitor."

Before Conti could answer, the newcomer stepped over to Faith, bowed slightly, and extended a hand. "I am, Reyher Cherro. A pleasure to make the acquaintance of such a lovely lady."

"Lord Cherro, this is the Magaestra I told you about, remember?" Conti's voice softened and took on a tone that niggled the back of Faith's memory.

"Ah!" Cherro's delight nearly sparkled from him.

Faith had to bite back a smirk at the thought of a sparkly vampire. Still, the word fit. Cherro was almost gleeful.

"It has been so long since I last tasted mage blood! Magaestra, hold still!" Faster than she could blink, Cherro held both her wrists in a firm grip over her head, his other hand pushing her shoulder down, and she was staring into the nearly black eyes of the vampire who had helped almost exterminate her kind.

"Master Cherro! Wait!" Conti's voice cracked out and then he was there, gently restraining Cherro as well. "She still has the drugs in her blood. You would get ill." His explanation was given in that softer voice again. It was almost as if he spoke to a young child, or–

"Drugs?" Cherro looked confused, and in almost any other situation Faith would have been amused by that expression on the face of such a lethal predator. "I don't like the way they taste, why would you let her have any drugs?"

"We needed to get her here in the first place, Master," Conti explained gently. "One of our mercenaries brought her in, unconscious. I was simply monitoring her until she regained consciousness. I wanted to ensure that she wasn't damaged."

Cherro chuckled. "You always do enjoy that part, old friend. The moment of realization in their eyes." He stood, releasing his hold on Faith who stayed very still, watching the interaction and hoping to draw no attention at all. Something about this interaction was very familiar, but with her heart racing and her adrenaline pumping, she couldn't quite place it.

Conti drew Cherro away a few steps and the conversation continued in murmured German until an older man hurried into the room. "There you are, sir! You told me you were fetching a book from the library, yet here you are chatting away in the sitting room. I cannot anticipate your needs if I can't even find you!"

The newcomer was tiny compared to the two vampires in front of her. If Faith had been casting for 'elderly caretaker' roles, then this new guy would have been near the top of her list.

"Reyher, did you escape your aide?" Conti's smile turned amused and teasing. "You know he is here to make your life easier, he cannot do that if you keep evading him!"

"He is the pushiest aide I have ever had. Regulating my meals and my schedule. Bah! I am his superior officer, not the other way around!" Cherro declared. His face was human again, and he pouted. It was fascinating to watch this interaction.

The most dangerous being here, possibly on the whole planet, and he was pouting at an old man about schedules and assistants.

"True, true," Conti chuckled. "But you know how many armies run on the backs of their aides."

Cherro sighed; a drawn-out, long-suffering sound. He muttered something in German again, and the only thing that stood out to Faith was the name *Wilhelm*. He then nodded and turned, and allowed the older man to lead him out of the room. Conti watched them go and Faith took the chance to move.

She tried to be quiet as she pulled her arms back down and sit up, but it was a struggle, making her limbs move the way she wanted them to. Whatever they had drugged her with was proving tough for her to shake completely off.

Conti turned back to her with what she could only describe as a predatory smirk. "You have a short reprieve since the chemicals in your bloodstream taste vile.

Drugged humans make for terrible meals, even if they have magic."

Faith glared at him.

"Oh, do you think you can fight us off? We know very well how to avoid your magical wrath. You don't think my good friend could feast on so many of you mages without learning a few tricks, did you? Besides, thanks to my new power, we have had to fireproof this whole complex while I learned how to control it."

"Fireproof?" The word popped out before Faith could stop it.

"Indeed! I could not have thought of a more flexible, delightful set of skills to start with! Your sister is delicious."

His grin now was slightly demented, but Faith couldn't care. Her stomach was again trying to heave whatever was left inside onto the floor and her body felt like ice. She couldn't think about it.

Faith dragged her thoughts back to the present moment from the panicky grief that threatened her and realized that Conti was still talking as if nothing he said was horrifyingly wrong.

"Although Reyher was not similarly affected. Curious that he gained no new skills. We are still trying to understand that, but I suspect he has simply built up a slight tolerance for the levels of magic in one mage. Like any other medication, probably. I shall have to discuss it with his doctor again." Conti was mostly talking to himself now, and Faith tried tapping into her magic again, but even though her mind was clearing up, her connection to her magic was still just as slippery as it had been when she first woke.

"At any rate, he has enough of his own powers. Do you have any idea who that man is? One of the greatest vampires to ever live, Reyher Cherro was one of the vampires who came so close to successfully gaining us our rightful place as masters of this world." His voice was full of admiration for the man who had just been ushered out, muttering petulantly in German.

"The whining guy? *That* guy is a great man?" Faith was going to get herself killed. She was usually much more level-headed in a crisis than this. Mouthing off at a homicidal lunatic was *not* level-headed. To be fair she had never been drugged and kidnapped by a vampire bent on world domination. This was a lot different than changing a flat tire or getting someone to the hospital after tripping on loose computer cables.

Conti's eyes flashed and a wave of pressure hit her skin, and her brain started to panic. Fight or flight didn't even begin to play into her thought process because the *presence* in the air was so strong that there was no way she could even hope to escape the predator it rolled off.

Faith remembered this feeling from the fight at the lodge. First Aldric had used it against the wolf in the front room, then one of the attacking vampires had tried to use it against her but it had been a weak effort compared to Aldric. This, though? This terrified her and she couldn't stop the panicked whimper that escaped her. A smile finally spread across Conti's face.

"Now you see," Conti leered at her. He resumed his seat and picked up the glass to drain the last of the blood. The back of her mind told her that the stuff had to be cold and congealing by now. "You will be respectful, Magaestra. We are superior to you in every way, and you will learn your place."

She shivered and this time it wasn't the cold seeping into her bones that caused it. Faith didn't say it but she would absolutely die first before she ever bowed and scraped to these people, or let them use her to further their own agendas. But she needed to live long enough to tell Aldric and Marc what she had learned. And she had learned several things.

The first thing she realized is that Crissy was almost certainly dead, or very close to it– although Cherro had mentioned another human here more than once, so she was going to cling to that hope.

The second thing she learned was that Cherro was not the one in charge here after all. Cherro was... senile? Whatever the vampire version of dementia was, Cherro seemed to be firmly in the grip of it. And Conti? Conti was both completely insane and desperate to help Cherro.

And she had to do everything she could to stay alive and relatively whole until Aldric and the rest of the Frost-walkers found her.

CHAPTER 15

Aldric was glaring out the front window considering putting GPS trackers on each of the vehicles and Marc was on the phone again, talking to a tracker out near the Latham's cabin. They had sent a team there and another out to where the Goldfang's camp had been, in the hopes that there would be something, any kind of clue to give them a direction to look.

"I have something," Leo's voice broke through Aldric's musings.

"I'll call you back, Jee. Thanks." Marc hung up and swiveled to face his screen. Aldric stepped behind him and they both waited for Leo to continue.

"Well, Addison found it this morning before we heard, and we doubled down on looking into it. I didn't want to say anything and get your hopes up or send anyone out on a wild goose chase." Leo grimaced.

"That explains your distractedness when we spoke," Marc nodded. "I thought you got a little extra distant after you stopped cussing."

Leo nodded. A voice from off-screen shouted, "Hurry up and *tell them*!"

Aldric raised an eyebrow when Leo's ears pinked, and under any other circumstances would likely have teased his cousin. It was good that one of them seemed destined for an easier time.

"She found an old written log of the mine system. I'll cut to the important bit, I think we found where the main Goldfang-vampire force is." Leo grimaced. "I sincerely doubt it's Alpha Molin in charge of it over there. We've gone through a ton of security footage and records and so on, and there's a warehouse complex that was bought recently by a company that is owned by a South American corporation that is, essentially, owned by Night's Phoenix Coven. Meaning, ultimately, it's owned by Reyher Cherro.."

Leo brought up a map and displayed it for them. "Here's the warehouse."

A circle appeared around a huge building surrounded by woods on two sides, a rocky ridge backing up behind the building. The last side was a wide, flat, weed-strewn field that had likely once been a parking lot.

"Where is it?" Aldric growled.

"Slow your roll, cuz," Leo sighed. "There's a bit more. That warehouse backs up onto a mine exit. A pretty big one, too. For a while that was one of the main mine entrances, then when the mine closed down, the ware-house owners used part of the caves as extra storage. That's why the building backs up so close. They could just drive right in and out of the mountain."

"What does that mean?" Marc asked. There was a hint of a growl in his voice, as well, which helped Aldric control himself. Simply knowing that his friend was as eager to shut Cherro down was a comfort.

"It means that this entrance has a connecting route to the cave Faith and Aldric fell into last week as well as a few others. We've been tracking down all the traffic around those locations and there's been an increase in truck traffic at two of them. Also..." Leo's face in the little box in the corner of the screen turned pensive. He grimaced and pulled his lip in to chew on it and glanced offscreen, likely at Addison.

"We found an old security system in the warehouse. It's not actually active anymore, and it's pretty ancient, technologically speaking, but it's still plugged in and connected up to everything. So I could hack into it."

Aldric tried to stay still and wait for what Leo was about to tell him.

"Um. I found confirmation that Cherro is there. And a *ton* of weapons and stuff. There're a few areas blocked off with drapes, and I can't see into them, but they look like they're set up as living spaces. I can see a part of a carpet and the edge of some sort of furniture. A chair or something. Cherro went in there a while ago, then came out escorted by an older man. I also caught a glimpse of Molin and a bunch of Goldfangs, and a lot of vampires are wandering around, doing whatever it is they're doing."

Marc took a deep breath and let it out slowly.

"How many would you guess were there guarding the place? And do you have any confirmation that Faith is there? Or Crissy?"

Leo scrunched his face up and squinted at some window on his screen that he wasn't sharing.

"I'd guess the rest of the Goldfangs are there," Addison's voice said from off-screen. A moment later her face popped into view, hovering over Leo's left shoulder. "So that's at least a couple dozen wolves."

She reached over Leo's arm to smack his hand off

something, then there was the sound of a mouse clicking, and a video image popped up. Alpha Molin, standing in an enormous open space, only cut off by a wall of curtains hung off pipes that seemed to be tied up to ceiling girders somehow. He was surrounded by three other men, and they all seemed to be listening to something on the other side of the curtain, with expressions of rage on their faces. After a moment he snarled and stalked off out of the camera's range, followed by his thugs.

"That was about an hour ago. Once we hacked in I started recording everything," she said with a grin.

"Well, at least he doesn't seem content in his association with Cherro," Aldric observed.

"Yeah. There's been some activity in what I'd say were the Goldfang areas," she agreed. "I've been trying to find any evidence that Faith or Crissy are there, but I haven't seen anything yet. The cameras have no internal storage so if the sisters were there before we found the cameras..." she shrugged.

"I'm sending you guys what we have. Old blueprints and such. We also have a few solid guesses as to what is where. There's a pretty obvious armory, and the blighthounds are being kept in the caves, I think. Easier to contain them that way," Leo said.

"I'm going to get back to trying to nail down where our people are." Addison nodded and disappeared off camera again.

"She's been a superstar," Leo glanced after her. "She's the one that found the cameras and reactivated them."

"We will find a way to express our gratitude," Aldric nodded.

"I'm going to call one of the Council members that I talked to the other day. He seemed to think that the whole situation needed more attention and was inclined to send help if we needed it," Marc scrubbed a hand over his head. "I'd say that this warrants the help. Assuming it's not a mediator and some cash."

Aldric nodded. "I know some people who might be willing to assist in a fight. I don't often call in outsiders, but I speak to a few mercenaries to keep up to date on current news and possible issues coming our way."

"We can't afford to pay many mercs, but we will do what we can," Marc nodded.

"We need a plan."

Marc looked at the screen, then at Aldric. "I have a plan. We rid ourselves of those psychopaths once and for all and get Faith and Crissy back home where they belong. We're going to war."

CHAPTER 16

Aldric found that once he started moving, he was finally focused and calm. Changing his clothes into something more suitable for a fight stilled his whirling thoughts and let him find a channel for his anger and his fear. Faith would be coming home with him tonight. There was no other way this would end.

"I have arranged with Tamika to leave me and Lucy and two others here to guard the children and Greg." Uncle Eldridge leaned on the door frame, his expression grave. "This must end tonight. Cherro cannot be allowed to try again."

Aldric nodded. "We know."

Eldridge nodded and stayed silent as Aldric sorted through his knives and chose several.

"I expect you won't need the knives much. Your hunting instincts will emerge quickly against the other vampires," Eldridge tipped his head. "Though I suppose there will be the Goldfangs, as well. And the hounds."

"Indeed. I would rather have my knives and not need them."

"Over-prepared beats underprepared, I agree. And the caves?" Eldridge asked.

Aldric grimaced. "There isn't a great deal we can do about them. The warehouse backs up right onto the cave entrance, so we cannot block their retreat if they try that."

"You could send a team in from the other side, through the cave system."

Aldric slipped the last night into his ankle holster and straightened. "We don't know the caves well enough, nor do we know how long it would take to go through them. It would be foolish to send anyone in to possibly get lost or badly injured in a place we cannot reach easily. We will have teams waiting at the known exits, however, once the main assault is over."

Eldridge nodded again.

"Be careful, Aldric." Eldridge stepped forward to wrap his arms around Aldric's shoulders and squeezed him tightly. "Come back in one piece, nephew, and bring Faith with you."

"I will."

They stood like that for another moment, before straightening and grinning at each other.

"Uncle Aldric!"

Kaylee came barreling into the room and leaped at Aldric, barely slowing down to glance around.

"Miss Kaylee, what are you doing up here? I thought that you and Jake were to be working with Mr. Greg?" Aldric glanced over her head at Eldridge who nodded.

"I escaped because everyone is talking about Aunt Faith and Mommy and the bad guys and they said that you're going to go get them back and stop the bad guys and that it's scary and there's those horrible dog monsters there and I don't want you to go and get hurt, but I want my mommy." Kaylee's words were almost unintelligible by the end of her statement as she sobbed into his shoulder and squeezed his neck with all her six-year-old strength, which was surprisingly considerable.

Aldric shifted the girl in his arms and sat on the bed, putting her securely in his lap as she continued to soak his shirt. "Kaylee."

Aldric wasn't sure how to soothe her. He had to go, not only because he would be damned if he left Faith in the hands of men so vile, but also because it was his duty. It was his honor to keep his clan safe, and there was no possibility of safety as long as not only the Goldfang Stalkers harassed them, but also while those vampires hid on the edges of their territory.

It would be only a matter of time before Cherro decided to expand his influence through the Frostwalker Clan lands.

"Kaylee, sweet girl. I must go. You know my job is to protect the clan," he said after a few minutes.

She sniffled into his shoulder and nodded. "Uh-huh."

"Well, part of that is fighting the bad guys when they come," he continued. He ran his hand up and down her back and was relieved when her sobs started to slow as she listened to him. "Unfortunately, many paranormals feel that their strength makes them better than others. Human police can't stop those people, so it falls to me and people like me. And when people like the ones who took your mother show up, it is up to people like me to stop them, too."

Kaylee sniffled again and peered up at him, her face blotchy and her eyes swimming. "Uncle Marc was talking to someone on the phone when I went past his office. He was yelling about people not getting here in time. Nobody is going to help you?"

"There are people who want to help us but they are too

far away to get here in time to assist," Aldric answered. It was hard to tell a child that sometimes adults were not as helpful as they ought to be. "And there are people closer that could help but are afraid, or want to help but have no training. I do not think we will be entirely alone in this, however. And I have a secret, remember? The bad guys don't know about that."

Kaylee's eyes grew wide. "A secret? Like a secret weapon?"

Eldridge chuckled and she spun to look at him.

"It is a little like that, yes, Kaylee. Aldric has a secret power that your aunt Faith gave him. But it's very secret. Like the superpowers in the movie you and Jake showed me, remember?" He smiled.

Kaylee nodded. "Is it ice powers? He's already super fast and super strong, but he said all vampires are like that, so it can't be that."

"No, Miss Kaylee, it isn't ice powers. But it may help keep me from being injured if I use it well. I have been practicing, do you want to see?"

Eldridge cocked an eyebrow in question and Kaylee nodded. Aldric smiled to see the tears drying in her new excitement. "Okay, but you must promise to keep it a secret. You can't tell anyone, okay? Marc and Eldridge know, but nobody else."

"I promise!"

Aldric was happy to show off a little bit, to reassure this girl who had lodged herself as firmly into his heart as her aunt had. Kaylee was suitably impressed.

"We have assistance coming?" Aldric asked. He glanced at the chair he usually chose when discussing things with Marc but couldn't relax enough to sit.

Marc, for his part, grimaced. "We do, a few enforcers from the Sun Ridge pack and about a dozen soldiers from the coven on the other side of the state. The Ulfred Coven. Their Master served with the Allies as well, and it sounded like he might come himself to assist. But nobody else can get here in time to be useful. They coven soldiers should be here in two hours, Master Arthur said. The wolves should be here soon."

"Kaylee said that she overheard you speaking of the Council?"

Marc actually growled now. "It appears that the Council is moving to make themselves more useful. They have formed an investigative branch to support their judicial proceedings. However, they are based in Ohio, so it will take them at least a day to get here. They suggested that we wait, and let them handle the whole situation themselves." Marc snorted a laugh, but the sound carried no humor. "I hope she didn't hear my response to that. It was not fit for young ears. Or probably adult ears for that matter. Either way, they are sending people out to investigate, but we'll worry about them later."

Tamika stepped into the room, clothed similarly to Aldric in all black, her braids pulled back into a tight bun, the beads in them silenced. "The rest of the Enforcers are going over a few things with their teams, anyone that wasn't there for the Goldfang's camp raid. I just wanted to check in before I go do the same. Have we got a time frame yet?"

"As soon as the Ulfred Coven soldiers get here. Eldred

and Lucy are staying here with a few sentries, but they'll be in the basement, which is a bit easier to defend," Marc grimaced. "Greg has apparently turned the meeting room into a *movie theatre* with a projector and blanket forts and some other things. Because my giant TV isn't good enough."

Tamika laughed. "You know how hard it is to distract a bored kid. Sometimes it just takes a little novelty like a movie projected onto the wall and a temporary fort."

"I am reassured to know that they are being distracted so well. Kaylee is frightened." Aldric rubbed his fingers against the still-damp fabric of his shirt, reminding himself that it was not merely Faith who was depending on them.

Marc nodded. "Jake is mad at me that I won't let him come with. I told him that he had to stay with Kaylee to keep her safe and calm." His expression was a mixture of ruefulness and pride.

"I assume the mention of Kaylee did the trick?" Tamika smirked.

Marc nodded. "Yeah. And Lucy offered to teach him a few moves, quote 'to use against any bad guys foolish enough to take you on' end quote. I think I'm half in love with that woman."

Aldric found himself relaxing slightly, the last of the blind rage and panic seeping from his muscles. Marc and Tamika knew full well that he needed to be focused on his task when they left here.

"You might have to fight Eldridge for her if you want to pursue that, Chief. Those two have been chatting and grinning almost since she got here." Tamika turned a sly smile on Aldric. "Guess it runs in the family for these Latham ladies."

"I can't say I blame either of them," Marc grinned

himself. "They're both remarkable. I can't wait to meet Crissy."

"I doubt she is in any frame of mind to enter into a courtship, but the best of luck," Aldric said, keeping his tone dry. He was about to continue when the doorbell rang and they all tensed. A minute later, Rod stepped into the doorway.

"Enforcers from the Sun Ridge Pack, Chief Keller," Rod announced formally, then stepped aside. A tall, whippet-slim man with bright red hair stepped into the room wearing all black clothing and a cocky smirk.

"Chief Keller." He bowed slightly at Marc then flicked his glance between Tamika and Aldric, and nodded to them as well. "I am Redmond Stagg of the Sun Ridge Pack, and I hear you've got a slight psychopath infestation you'd like some help with."

"You heard correctly. We have two clanmates kidnapped by an alliance between the Goldfang Stalker Pack and the remains of the Immortal Thirst Coven."

Redmond whistled low. "Damn. I've always heard that when a Frostwalker does something they do it right. You sure don't go halfway with your enemies."

"I will not be lax in my destruction of them, either," Aldric growled.

Redmond blinked at him for a moment. "You must be Aldric Donnelly. I've never met a vampire warrior before, I look forward to seeing you in action."

Tamika snorted. "One of the kidnaped Frostwalkers is his girlfriend. Once we get there you're not likely to see anything but a trail of bodies once this one catches her scent."

Redmond looked delighted and clapped his hands together. "So we're not even pretending to play nice, then?

Excellent! I brought a dozen of our best fighters with me. What's our plan?"

"We can confirm details when the last of our allies arrive, but here is what we were thinking." Marc stood up and swiveled his monitor around to go over the plan and see where Redmond thought his people would do the most good.

CHAPTER 17

Faith shivered on the stupid chaise lounge that she sat on. Screw the expensive upholstery, she pulled her feet up to curl into a ball and conserve as much warmth as she could. Conti had left her sitting there without so much as a glass of water, let alone a blanket. A bored-looking man was playing on his phone a few feet away, presumably on babysitting duty.

The most insulting part was that if she wasn't so cold and hungry, she probably could have taken him out even without her magic. Tamika's self-defense lessons were no joke. But the cold of the space had seeped into her bones and she couldn't stop shivering. How long had she been here? It felt like hours. And she had no way to even guess how long she had been drugged unconscious for. Aldric and the clan *must* know she was missing by now.

Faith shivered and tried to use her magic again. She had been testing herself every so often, trying to keep alert and positive, and the magic was getting easier to hold on to. Hopefully, soon she could actually manipulate it again.

As long as she was alive, she could fight, after all. Somehow. If nothing else she could punch the shit out of those vampire jerks. The sudden memory of Cherro's hands squeezing her wrists flashed into her mind and she shivered for a completely different reason.

When Aldric saw those bruises he was going to go postal.

Okay, so *maybe* she could punch the vampire jerks. Either way, they weren't expecting her to fight back, especially if they thought her magic was suppressed. Which brought up another question: if they didn't want to feed until after whatever she was drugged with was totally out of her system, then how did they expect to get to her once she could use her shield again? Presumably, they were aware that the drug and her magic-less state were connected.

Her guard's phone beeped and he swiped at the screen. He grunted quietly before responding. Faith watched the man texting for a minute before he shrugged and stuffed his phone back in his pocket. He looked over at her and met her eyes for a long moment, his thoughts churning behind his gaze. Then he shrugged, turned, and silently walked out of the room.

Faith was alone.

She waited a long time, listening as hard as she could to the muffled sounds from the other side of the drapery walls, but all she heard was the scurrying of feet and a few canine claws on a concrete floor. Sitting here and waiting for someone to come back wasn't an option Faith wanted to explore, so, picking a direction she stood carefully.

Her legs didn't want to hold her up as easily as usual and she still shivered. Stiff and feeling a bit weak from the cold she stretched first, then headed to the corner of the room opposite from the opening in the curtains that served as a doorway. She stopped to listen again but there was only silence on the other side as far as she could tell.

It was a damn shame that her magic powers didn't come with enhanced senses like the rest of the paranormal world got. *Well, my choices are to take a chance out there or wait in here for Crazy Vampire One and Crazy Vampire Two to come back,* she grumbled to herself. Ducking low, she peeked between the edges of the curtain wall near door level.

What she was, it turned out, was a warehouse. A huge one, apparently split down the middle, with one side mostly clear floor with a few crates and a forklift along one stretch of wall, and tall rows of industrial shelving occasionally interspersed with more curtains. More living spaces, she guessed.

The corner she was in was where the curtains were hung from the shelves and went back to the actual wall, but there was just enough space between the boxes on the bottom row of the nearest shelf for her to squeeze out. It reminded her a little bit of playing hide and seek with Crissy in the giant Ikea warehouse when they were still kids.

And that was another question. Conti had implied that Crissy was here somewhere. Or another human mage, at the very least, but Faith was hoping he meant her sister. A plan started to form in her mind to search the rooms for her sister and get her out as well.

She crept from one shelf to another, hiding behind boxes and crates where they were shoved into the storage. It wouldn't really help her, with both the Goldfang wolves and the vampires able to track her scent, but it had to be better than being out in the open.

She reached another curtain and peeked through the

corner. It seemed to be set up as a dining room with a highly polished wood table and fancy padded chairs. Lining the edges of the room was a long, low cabinet that Faith imagined would be used as a serving station or a buffet, and a tall breakfront full of what she could only assume was very expensive china and crystal. The whole room screamed expensive and sumptuous in a very old-fashioned, eighties TV drama sort of way.

The weird taste of the decorator wasn't her concern. What Faith cared about was that it was empty, since she had to cross it to get to the other curtain wall. She stayed low and made a dash for it, crouching behind the buffet and crept out.

She had to do some careful shoving and twisting to get past the crates on the other side of the dining room curtain wall. She took a moment to read over a shipping label as she squeezed by and recognized it as the same as the labels on the crates they had removed from the Goldfang's camp a few days earlier.

Which meant that these shelves held weapons. A ton of weapons. And explosives, if she remembered right. Oh hell. Faith stifled a growl– she really had been spending time with wolves– and made a note to herself to tell Aldric and Marc when she got free.

The place was enormous, and the number of shelves felt endless. Faith ducked through two more rooms- the library she remembered someone mentioning and what seemed like a kitchen of sorts. She took a moment to peek into the fridge and found it was sectioned, with half of the shelves full of gourmet brands of food and the other half stacked with enough blood to feed an army, if everyone fed like Aldric did only every few days.

Pity, she didn't have time to cook anything, but she snagged some bread and ate quickly as she moved on.

She slunk through another section of shelves and breathed deeply before peeking through the next curtain. It took her a minute to figure out what she was looking at: the metal and plastic base of a hospital bed, with all the plugs and wires that seemed to involve snaking along the floor past where she rested her fingers.

Faith frowned to herself and peered further into what she could see of the room. It wasn't set up as a fancy living space like the others— even the kitchen had a high-end, expensive feeling to it— but what she imagined a prison medical center might be. There was another bed she could see part of, made up neatly and ready for use with hand-cuffs dangling from bars running up the side, and a large refrigerator with a giant lock on it. She couldn't see anything else, but a glance down the outside of the curtains told her that the room wasn't huge, but had enough space for three or four beds.

What would they need an infirmary for? As far as Faith knew, none of the people they sent after the Frostwalkers lived to get back here for medical treatment. Well, the ones that did survive end up in Marc's rogue wolf cells, and that wasn't all that many prisoners. So what—

The answer hit her and she felt sick. Blood collection. In hindsight it was obvious, but she could argue with herself later. Right now she had to listen very carefully to the inside of that room before going in and breaking her sister out.

Silence. Nothing but muffled silence and the occasional hum of equipment. Faith peeked back into the room and listened again without the fabric muffling sounds. Still, no indication that anyone was in the room, not even Crissy, though it made the most sense so far. There weren't exactly a lot of holding cells in this giant, open space, and curtain walls were not exactly as secure as a cell at Alcatraz.

She crept in, crawling next to the bed frame that blocked her view, and peered around the end. She had guessed right. Three beds and one bigass refrigerator. There was some other equipment sitting next to the bed opposite her that Faith assumed was for involuntary blood donations, and a smaller version of the industrial shelves surrounding them, loaded down with smaller boxes of gauze and medical tape and needles, and other assorted supplies. There was no desk or anything else.

Taking a chance, she stood up and immediately focused on the last bed in the room.

"Crissy!" Faith only just remembered to keep her voice down, so the word came out as a choked-back whisper, but it still felt as loud as a shout in the silence. Hopefully, the curtains muffled the noise.

Crissy didn't answer, just sighed, and kept her eyes closed. She was pale-- very pale-- and her hair lay limp and greasy on the pillow. She was handcuffed to the bed on one side, and her other arm was folded over her belly on top of a thin, wrinkled blanket.

Faith hurried over to her sister, her blood boiling. "Crissy, I'm here." Faith grabbed her sister's hand making the handcuff clink. Her anger rose at how cold her sister's hand was.

"Faith?" Crissy whispered. Her eyelids fluttered and then opened and Faith vowed that Conti and Cherro wouldn't breathe much longer if she had anything to say about it. Her sister's eyes, usually a warm brown and sparkling with humor were muddy and dull.

"Faith you have to run. These people. they're--"

"I know, Cris. But I'm not leaving without you. Kaylee would kick my butt."

Crissy's grip tightened slightly. "Is she here?"

Faith shook her head. "No. She's back at the Frostwalker clan house. If I know those guys, your baby girl won't be able to sneeze without three enforcers and a few sentries right there to offer her a tissue. They have to have realized I'm missing by now."

Crissy clutched at Faith's hand. "Do you swear that she's safe there? Swear to me, Faith. These monsters. They're..." Crissy's voice broke.

"I told you at the lodge. The Frostwalkers are good people. They'll protect Kaylee with their lives if they have to," Faith smiled sadly. "One of them already has, in fact. Kaylee is as safe as she can be. And Aunt Lucy showed up. I promise, paranormal or not, nobody's going to want to go up against her. Hold tight."

Faith eased her hand out of her sister's grip and bent to the ground. Thank all that was holy that the arrogant idiots hadn't taken her shoes off when they tossed her purse. Faith remembered laughing at Tamika as the Enforcer snatched them one day and started prying at the soles.

"You never know when a few extra tools'll come in handy, sugar!" Tamika had grinned at Faith, who rolled her eyes at the time.

"Remind me to thank Tamika. And apologize for not believing her," she muttered. She stood and winked at her sister, flashing the thin metal tool. "I told her I'd never need this thing or the knowledge of how to use it, but she insisted on teaching me."

"You gotta have faith," Crissy muttered back and Faith's heart soared to hear the familiar, terrible old joke. Crissy may be down, but she wasn't out.

Feet pounded past the open doorway just as the cuff clicked and released Faith peeked out the corner of the curtains to see the last of a group of men flash down the warehouse. Did that mean they were heading to the exit or to the back of the warehouse? Was there an exit on both ends? She hadn't been in many warehouses, but it seemed reasonable. One end of the place was visibly closer than the other.

"What do you mean the wolves are gone?" Conti's voice bellowed from somewhere near the far end where the group had disappeared, making her decision on which way to go. "That idiot Alpha swore his fealty!" He followed that up with what Faith could only assume was some creative cursing in Spanish.

"Shit. I think our grace period just ran out. Can you sit up?" Faith bent to put her tools away. "I'm just glad this handcuff was a cheap one. I'm not sure I'm good enough to crack something serious. I doubt those assholes expected old-fashioned lockpicking."

"I'm dizzy, sis. And really weak. They've been taking blood every day. And those monsters bi-- bit me." Faith didn't miss the hitch in Crissy's words.

"Killing them once won't be nearly enough." Faith carefully pushed her arm under Crissy's shoulders and helped her sit up, then a moment later to stand slowly.

"Dizzy," Crissy muttered.

A sound that Faith imagined was what gave rise to the myth of the banshee shot through the building, making her hair stand on end. It was horrifying, a sound of rage and promise death, but instead of causing terror Faith found herself grinning as a wave of pure power washed over her skin.

"Aldric. He's here."

A wave of similar, but less potent shrieks answered Aldric's hunting cry and unleashed power buffeted her awareness, but it was when two louder, powerful cries joined the response that Faith shook herself and got moving. She wrapped Crissy's arm around her shoulders and helped her trembling sister start moving just as a chorus of howls and shrieks rose again from outside.

"Lean on me. We're getting out of here."

CHAPTER 18

Aldric crouched in the brush that edged the property and peered through the binoculars Marc handed to him. He watched Molin and about two dozen wolves storm out of the warehouse and into vehicles and drive off.

"Where do you think they're headed?" Marc asked.

Aldric just shook his head. If they were heading to the clan house they were going to have a very disappointing welcome. Eldridge, Lucy, and an entire team of sentries stayed behind to guard the children. Tamika had taken Lucy to the basement gym for some friendly sparring the day before and assured him that anyone who tried to get past the older human would regret their assumptions of automatic superiority very quickly.

"Leo, The Goldfangs seem to have left the building. Keep an eye on those idiots if you can, would you?" Marc had his phone out. They didn't have fancy communication devices like the ones that were so popular in the movies. They had never had a need for them and while Leo was an excellent hacker, but he was no gadget genius, conveniently coming up with exactly what they needed.

"Great, thanks. And give the folks at the house a heads up that they might have company. Molin might try to hit the house while we're not there." He heard Marc stuff his phone back in his pocket, then turn to Aldric, who was still peering through the binoculars. "See anything else?"

"There is that slight space between the ridge and the warehouse that we noticed on the images Leo provided. It does seem well wide enough for a body to fit through, and even if it is not, I can without a more solid form. But I foresee no difficulty on that score." Aldric didn't elaborate. They had planned a similar strategy to their raid on the Goldfang's camp: there was a team positioned near the back of the warehouse intending to cut off any possible escape through the caves, and they intended to use that gap for their entry.

Aldric hoped he wouldn't need to use his new skill, but considering Cherro had fed on countless mages in the past, he suspected there was only a very slim chance of keeping his new secret. It was likely that after this battle the Ulfred Coven and the Sun Ridge Pack would know that the Frost-walkers hosted a human mage, and also know about Aldric's own new abilities. That would bring a whole different set of problems upon them.

If Marc didn't trust them, then they wouldn't be here, he reminded himself, and in truth, Aldric found he cared somewhat less than he likely thought. By the end of today, the Frostwalker Clan would have eliminated this coven and two of the most dangerous creatures to walk the Earth, and possibly the Goldfang Stalkers Pack as well, thus proving to the world that they would fiercely protect their own. There were no alternatives. Either they took Faith and Crissy home today or Aldric would be past caring about it.

And he was not dying while Faith was still endangered.

"You are growling, friend. And prepared for battle already." The Master of the Ulfred Coven slid up beside Aldric. "She is that important to you?"

Aldric couldn't hear any mockery in the man's tone so he simply nodded.

"Then we will get her back and end this," the other vampire said. Aldric felt a hand rest on his shoulder.

"Congratulations, Enforcer Donnelly. We will rescue your mate and put a final stop to this, as we should have back then. Nobody should go through what he likely has planned for her."

Aldric did lower the binoculars now to turn and stare, keeping his expression as neutral as he could. Master Arthur tipped his head and a smile flickered across his face.

"I am an intelligent man. As soon as you briefed us on who we were coming up against, and that he had one of your people, it was not a difficult connection to make." Master Arthur snarled now. "My father was a mage, and while I did not inherit any of his power, I am still connected to many who once hid those who were hunted, as well as a sadly dwindling number of mages. I will not allow this to continue. I only regret not bringing more of my warriors."

This was news to Aldric. Very few paranormals had human parentage for one reason or another. He could not offhand think of any other who had a human mage as a parent.

"Nobody should be hunted, not simply due to their birth." Master Arthur said, his face deadly serious. "But remember. She will likely not thank you for getting your-self killed in the process of freeing her."

Marc's rumbled growl of agreement from Aldric's other side reminded him that this was a bigger battle than simply him versus one or two rogues. He was ready for a fight now, and he had what felt like the world to protect. Faith and Crissy and Kaylee were Frostwalkers. They were his family. They would be home, safe, and comfortable by the end of the day.

"I wonder," Master Arthur. "Have you started to bond?"

Aldric felt his face start to heat but kept his expression neutral and held his tongue.

A twinkle appeared in Gregory's eye. "I ask because my parents were bonded, and I see the same sort of look about you. Not as strong, but, I wondered. I believe that if there is that connection between you, even just a thread of one, you may be able to sense approximately where she is in the building, and if we're lucky, a few other things. It will depend on several factors that I admit I am not very familiar with, but any information is good information before we move."

Aldric frowned. Master Arthur did not seem to have an ulterior motive for asking. Marc hummed on his other side.

"Might be useful to know where she is if we can find her. Leo still hadn't seen her on the cameras, when I just asked him."

Aldric turned his gaze to the warehouse. It was a huge building, meant to house mining equipment and trucks large enough to take huge amounts of rock and earth out to one of the enormous piles quickly turning into thickly forested hills around them.

He took a deep breath, closed his eyes, and searched in himself for a hint of Faith's bright soul. He knew that there would be a connection, whether or not they were forming a bond, but because Aldric could still feel her magic flowing through his veins with every beat of his heart, but he knew Lucy and Master Arthur were right, the bond was there. Thin and incomplete, but there.

It was that sense of her, of her magic that he focused on now, following the thread of power from his own body outward, toward the warehouse. It was probably no more than a few seconds but it seemed like an eternity as he stretched out his senses until he found her.

Frightened and determined and not *injured* but still not whole. Her magic seemed disconnected from her, somehow, and she was not pulling on it as he had expected.

Aldric was unsure how this bond worked. His own parents had been bonded, true, but they had never discussed it in any depth. He knew that they always had a sense of each other, however. Neither needed words to know the state of the other, and that was what Aldric hoped he could tap into now.

He sent reassurance, or he tried to, across the thin thread of their connection. There was no answering rise in her confidence, and Aldric doubted she could sense him. He did however hear a loud shout, too far and too muffled to make out the words, but it caused a spike of anxiety and fear in Faith.

That was intolerable. If she could not sense him through their connection, then he would let her know another way.

He lifted his chin and released a hunting cry that had birds lifting from trees for miles around. His power, the magic that sustained him as a vampire and fed his abilities swept out from him in an expanding ring, almost visibly making the air shimmer as it passed. He poured every ounce of his intention to destroy Cherro and Conti into his cry.

Beside him, Marc, Arthur, and the rest of their allies gasped in surprise and he could sense the vampires among their force responding to the cry by shifting fully into their fangs and claws.

A wave of power hit their force as the vampires in the warehouse answering his challenge. The Frostwolf warriors, as well as the Sun Ridge wolves and the Ulfred Coven vampires, raised their own voices, howling or shrieking their power as two distinct voices rose over the din from the warehouse

Cherro, he guessed, was prepared for them. And the other would be Conti, Aldric guessed.

He also sensed a surge of relief through the thready connection he was holding firm in his mind. Faith did not howl, as she had done several times before in their battles, though, and Aldric hoped it was not because she was injured.

Marc nodded and the tone of his howl changed to one of command. The battle was begun.

Aldric raced to the warehouse and made for the door in the long side of the building that was his team's targeted entry. It burst open and vampires charged out. They were not the thugs sent by Molin. These were trained and hardened soldiers, and they would not go down easily.

He led a team of his own sentries as well as the team of Sun Ridge wolves, and Redmond cackled with glee as he kept pace with Aldric right up to the line of vampires waiting for them. Hopefully, the man was as skilled as he was cocky. That was all Aldric had time to think before they engaged.

The stench of blood almost immediately blanketed the battlefield. Wolves snarled and vampires hissed, throwing their power out to try to intimidate the attacking force. The wolves only responded by fighting harder.

A shriek from near the front of the building told Aldric that there was a similar scene there, where Marc and Master Arthur led the assault. The last group was trying to enter the warehouse from the other side and were attempting to be quiet, and Aldric took reassurance that he heard nothing from there.

He tore through his opponent and moved on to the next, advancing ever closer to the doorway that would let him inside to search for Faith. He kept a firm lock on his anger at these vampires, these *vermin* who dared to consider themselves above those around them. He recalled something he was told once when he asked how anyone could stay calm in the face of the atrocities of war.

"You don't stay calm. You get angry. You get filled with an understandable rage at how callous one person can treat another, but you don't let that anger consume you or lead you. You take it and you use it as a tool. You focus your rage into a scalpel and cut out the evil of the world to save the good," his friend had said. Aldric took that advice to heart now and sliced through the defending vampires as if they barely resisted.

He turned to the last man between himself and the door and unleashed another wave of his power and the soldier paled, but stood firm. At least until Aldric took the man's head from his shoulders with one slice of his claws. Uncle Eldridge had been right. He had yet to even pull out a knife.

"Clear this infestation then follow me inside," he shouted to his people. He got growls and battle cries in response, and he heard one of the sentries shout "Bring Faith home, boss!"

With a nod, he turned to the door. When he stepped inside the dim space he felt a wave of panic hit him and he heard Faith's scream.

He roared his challenge. Shelves rattled and dust rained down from the girders above with the sound, and it wasn't a second before he had found her. She was huddled near a towering metal shelf with someone behind her, her arms up to hold a shield firm, looking so much like she had when he first met her that his chest squeezed. But it wasn't a half-rogue wolf that was trying to break through to her this time.

"Sandalio Conti." The name came out as a hiss, his fangs prominent enough now to hamper his speech. He had to be careful, though, because where Conti was, Cherro must be nearby.

The man turned at the sound of his name and hissed, sending his power out to try to intimidate Aldric into a mistake, but it barely felt like more than a flicker in his awareness. The man was powerful, strong, and had certainly fed on a mage— the human magic was prominent in his power.

"Aldric! Watch out!" Faith shouted as the other vampire rushed at him and he had no time for anything but the fight.

CHAPTER 19

aith got Crissy out of the medical room and down three aisles of shelving before she ran into her first major problem.

"Where is the Magaestra?" Conti's voice echoed through the warehouse. Outside the sounds of fighting were getting louder and Faith knew it was just a matter of time before her friends could get to her. It would no doubt help them, though, if she could get herself and Crissy some place safe. Somewhere to their left, from what she imagined was the back of the warehouse, the snarls of blighthounds sounded way too loud for her comfort.

"Shit. Shit shit shit." She muttered.

"I don't know what those things are, but if I never see one again I'll be okay with that," Crissy muttered.

"Agreed," Faith nodded. She peered around the box they crouched by and her eyes snagged on a door. It was across the wide-open side of the warehouse, with nothing to screen them from anyone's sight, but it was probably their best chance. And, strangely, Faith felt a pull in that direction as if that door, specifically, somehow represented more safety than any other option.

Not that they had any other options, really.

"Okay, sis. Put as much as you can into this. I'll try to carry you as best as I can, but you have to help, okay?" Faith said, keeping her voice low. There was a ripping noise and a crash, and she realized that Conti was following her trail. "*Shit!* Okay, Cris. We're going to that door as fast as we can."

"There's vampires freaking everywhere!" Crissy's eyes were huge and darting around.

"Yeah, but none of them are paying attention to us. They're all more worried about the attack outside. Conti is the one we have to get away from." And with that she pulled Crissy up, and half dragged her down the aisle to the open side of the warehouse.

The crashing behind them grew closer and Faith tried to pick up the pace, but Crissy was still a full-grown woman and Faith was still just Faith. She scrabbled for her magic to try to get some help. If she could levitate Crissy, even a little…

"*You!*"

She was out of time. The damn door was so close, but there was no way she could beat vampire speed, even if she wasn't carrying her sister.

"Did you think you could escape *me?*" Conti bellowed. His eyes were almost fully black and his whole face was sharper. He hissed, pulling his lips back and flashing those deadly fangs. "I am Sandalio Conti! Right hand of Reyher Cherro and we will *rule!* You are *nothing!*"

"I am Faith Latham, Magaestra of the Frostwalker Clan, and what you are is a psychotic asshole!" Maybe taunting the psychotic asshole wasn't the healthiest of options, but if anyone needed to be called on his bullshit it was this guy. "Your side lost almost a hundred years ago, and you're about to lose again."

She got her mental fingers around her magic and *pulled* just as he rushed toward them. Her shield flared brightly around them, a bubble of pure, solid magic, and Conti snarled in frustrated rage.

"You will die slowly!" he hissed. "I will keep you alive and aware for *years* as I drain you to power my army!"

"Something tells me that isn't going to happen." Her magic flared with recognition and she couldn't stop the grin if she'd had to.

"Faith! What are you *doing?* Don't make him even angrier! He's crazy!" Behind her Crissy grabbed her shirt and clung to it as they both folded toward the floor. Faith was dizzy again, the fog from when she first woke up teasing the edges of her vision, but she kept her grip on the magic and brought both hands up to brace the shield.

The door behind Conti, the one she had been trying to reach, for slammed open just then and she had never seen a more glorious sight in her life. There, silhouetted by bright daylight, was Aldric. He was more fully vampire than she had ever seen him, his face was chalk-white and against that his dark hair and vampiric eyes resembled what she imagined a black hole looked like. They just absorbed the light and didn't reflect any.

"Sandalio Conti," he hissed. She could see his fangs from here, some twenty feet away, and that, too was stunning. Faith's brain bubbled up with the idle thought that maybe she should get some therapy if the sight of Aldric like this, crashing in like some sort of avenging demon, was the hottest thing she had ever seen in her life.

Conti whipped around at the sound of his name and Faith could feel his power crash over her, like fire ants all over her skin. Behind her Crissy whimpered.

Fiery sparkles danced behind Conti's back, and Faith had just enough time to cry "Aldric, look out!" before the two vampires were clashing together.

They moved way too fast for Faith to see, just two blurs to her eyes, but the snarls and hisses and blasts of power battered against her.

"Faith," Crissy's voice was more of a whisper than a real question as she clung to the back of Faith's shirt.

"It's going to be fine now, Cris. Aldric is here, and that means the rest of the Frostwalkers are, too." The women both flinched as a roaring challenge came echoing down the warehouse from what seemed to be the back.

"It's going to be fine, " Faith said again, making sure her voice was firm and confident. She didn't take her eyes off the blurring movement that was Aldric and Conti. Snarls and hisses punctuated the blurs, and Conti taunted Aldric with threats to the Frostwalkers Clan, Aldric's family, and Faith herself. It felt like the fight lasted for hours.

The vampires separated as Conti went stumbling backwards a few steps. Cheers from the other side of the door rose and the voices of wolves sang through the air and the clamor from behind them increased. Both vampires were covered in blood. Aldric's black t-shirt hung in two long flaps, clinging to the bloody edges of what must be claw wounds under the smears of blood. Conti's elegant suit was in tatters and he held his left arm stiffly against himself.

"You and your fleabags won't stop us," Conti snarled. "You may win this fight, perhaps, but we *will* take our rightful place. Vampires belong at the top, and you know it, Donnelly."

Aldric said nothing. Behind her Crissy whimpered as another wave of power crashed into them from somewhere else, oily feeling and tainted somehow. Aldric snarled in response to the sound and his own power felt soothing and gentle to Faith as it brushed away both Cherro's and Conti's efforts, but Conti flinched back again.

Conti's gaze flickered to the women huddled on the floor and his expression changed slightly.

"The woman is important to you, personally, I understand," Conti's voice was enticing and soft now. He took a small step closer to Aldric, who stood like a stone wall. "How about a compromise. You can join us, keep the woman to feed from yourself. We can store her blood for distribution easily enough, but she can stay in your quarters."

No response from Aldric. He just stood there, breathing heavily, his blood-darkened eyes watching, waiting.

"Don't you want to be on the side of those that rule the world? Cherro will recover and his rule will be glorious!"

Conti took another step forward. Something at the side of Faith's vision flickered, and she tore her gaze away from the confrontation in front of her to look. Sparks of fire wove around and through the boxes behind Aldric, white hot and silent.

"Aldric, look out!"

She flung a hand out to wrap her shield around his exposed back in time for the sparks of fire to crash into it, stinging burns into her palm as the magics clashed. She saw Aldric glance back as he stepped away from Conti's magic attack, and the other vampire hissed, thwarted for a second before crowing in delighted victory. Faster than she could track, he was in front of her, grabbing her by the hair and dragging her close to his body.

She could smell the stale blood on his breath when he leaned close and licked up the side of her neck.

"No wonder you want to keep this one!" His voice was gleeful and she tried to cringe away when he went to lick her again, but his grip on her hair was too tight, and he had his other arm wrapped tightly around her. Faith couldn't remember any of Tamika's lessons now, as terror and disgust fought for control of her brain.

"Let. Her. Go." Aldric's voice was inhuman. "This is your only chance."

"You have lost. I will feed on her then kill you, then I will take care of the rest of those mutts," Conti gloated. He moved to bite down on the flesh he had exposed before him, but something warm and soft hit her skin instead. She peeled her eyelids open-- when had she squeezed them closed?-- and looked around as well as she could in Conti's unforgiving grip, but she couldn't see his face through the fog that surrounded him.

"What—?" Conti's voice was muffled through the thick white cloud, but she could hear him sputtering and gasping. His grip loosened and she yanked back, stumbling when she was freed. Crouching by Crissy and automatically shielding them again, as her sister clung to Faith and sobbed, they watched in shock as Conti staggered and tried to claw at the mist that covered his head.

She would never be able to say how long she and her sister held each other, crouched behind her shield, watching Aldric suffocate Conti, but in the end, the once elegant zealot lay still on the concrete floor and Aldric crouched over him, stone-faced, and punched his claws into Conti's chest to pull out the other vampire's heart.

Crissy whimpered as Conti started to shrivel and even Faith shuddered to watch it happen. She had seen dead vampires before, but she had never seen one age in front of her like this. And she had never seen Aldric kill so coldly. He dropped the wrinkled husk that was once Conti's heart on top of the pile of shredded, bloody clothes wrapped around the desiccated corpse and stood.

When he turned his gaze on Faith, she felt Crissy yanking on her shirt, almost overbalancing her. Aldric closed his eyes and took a deep, slow breath in. He repeated the process twice, three times. Then as he blew his breath out again, his features softened, his skin took on more color, and she watched in fascination as his clawed fingers shrank and rounded.

She blinked up at him and he stepped over to crouch in front of her, the corner of his lip twitching as he peered at the air between them where her shield still sat.

"You saved me," Aldric murmured. "Again."

Faith swallowed and lowered her hand, the shield fading. A wave of dizziness hit her and she wobbled on her knees, only to be caught in Aldric's arms. She glanced up at him, his lips definitely pulling up at the corners now.

"We must stop meeting like this, Magaestra. It is becoming a habit," he said.

"Yeah, well. At least it wasn't rogue werewolves this time?" Faith said, fighting her own grin. How they could joke like this was beyond her ability to understand and frankly, she didn't have the energy to worry about it.

"You are safe now. Both of you." His eyes flicked up to include Crissy in the promise. "Our clan is here, as well as allies from a nearby coven and a neighboring pack sent a number of their enforcers. Conti is dead and Cherro will not live much longer either, if Master Arthur has not already ended his life. There will be none left to lead this faction. You will be safe."

"And when you get hungry? Will we be safe then?" Crissy asked. She lifted her chin, but Faith could see the trembles in her shoulders, and feel them through where Crissy still clung to her shirt.

"Magaestra, there is nothing I can say that will assure you. I understand that it will take time for you to judge me by my actions, but I swear to you, as the Head Enforcer for the Frostwalker Clan, and as a Donnelly, you will be protected."

"Cris, he's a good man. You can trust him. I'll tell you all about everything, but first, can we please get out of here?" Faith looked up at Aldric as she asked the last question, and he smiled. Just as he nodded there was a piercing howl, and dozens of voices picked up the cry.

"Cherro is dead." Aldric smiled.

Faith grinned and tipped her head back over his arm and let her own voice join the chorus, which caused a surge in volume as her clanmates heard her and knew she was safe.

CHAPTER 20

Faith heartily hoped that this was the last time she spent the night with someone in a hospital bed.

Okay, so it was really one of the guest rooms in the clan house, and super comfortable, but still. Crissy lay in the bed with an IV hooked up, dripping whatever it was Madeline had gone on about the night before. As it turned out, aside from being weakened from having her blood collected at far too frequent intervals and being underfed, Crissy was actually in relatively decent shape, so that was a massive relief.

She had nightmares, though, and wound up sleeping with Kaylee on one side of her, Faith on the other side, carefully leaning on the bed from a chair to avoid tangling the IV line, and a puppy Jake curled up on her knees. Both Marc and Aldric checked in regularly, which Faith knew because she barely slept at all.

Madeline bustled in and patted Faith's shoulder.

"It's four in the morning. You should go to bed and get some real sleep," she said when Faith sat back to let the doctor close enough to look over the equipment.

"I can't..." Faith started to object.

"Faith. For your own health. You need rest. You had a pretty traumatic day yesterday and you need to recover as well." Madeline crouched down to look Faith right in the eye. "Crissy will be fine. She is safe and sound, and will probably be resting for another day or two, but nobody with ill intent is going to get anywhere close to her. Rod is right outside, and I know Lucy and Eldridge are going to bring in breakfast in a few hours. You can be back for that."

"She's right, sis. Go get some sleep." Crissy's voice was quiet but much stronger than it had been just the night before. A look of hesitation and nerves crossed her face when she glanced at Madeline but was quickly replaced with determination. "I'll be fine. I've got the best guard dog available here, so don't worry, okay?" Crissy grinned down at the soft lump of fur that was Jake, who was wiggling around to flop half on Kaylee's ankles just to huff back into little puppy snores.

It took another ten minutes to convince Faith to head back to her room. Rod, lounged against the wall right across the hall from Crissy's door, as Madeline had said.

"I'll keep her safe. I promise you." His giant frame and bald head made him look more than a little intimidating, but he smiled at her and his blue-grey eyes crinkled at the corners, making him look a little like a biker elf.

"I know. I just..."

"You just got your sister back after weeks of stress and worry and fighting. The adrenaline and the anxiety won't let go easily, but they will. Get some rest and a few meals into you, spend some time with Aldric and then come back to your sister. She'll be here. I won't leave her alone, even if I have to shift and catch a nap on the floor, okay?" Rod winked at her. "Jake's not the only good guard dog around, you know. Kenya and Ori are just down the hall sleeping until it's their shift on watch, and Tamika's downstairs prowling around. Marc and Aldric are also still on alert since we haven't tracked down Molin yet. We've got you."

Faith rolled her eyes at him, but then ducked in and hugged him tight.

"Thanks, Rod," she said into his chest.

"Anytime." He patted her shoulder. "Now go on and get a little snack, grab a nice hot shower, and get some rest. You'll feel about a thousand times better."

Faith stepped back and nodded. "I will. Thanks."

Faith made her way down to the kitchen, stumbling on the last step, but she made it under her own steam and was weirdly proud of that. The light was on and a figure sat at the kitchen table, his back to her. It wasn't a familiar back, and Faith paused just outside the door, wondering if she should just go to bed and eat later.

She was about to turn around when the man tipped his head, then turned to look at her. She vaguely remembered him from the warehouse. He had helped the Frostwalkers keep a clear path while Aldric and some wolves she didn't know got her and Crissy to an SUV and away from that awful place.

"Good morning, Magaestra," he said. his voice was pitched low, probably to avoid waking anyone else in the house. It was stupid o'clock a.m. after all. Sane people were asleep.

"Um, morning," Faith answered. She hesitated for another moment then stepped into the kitchen. It was her home, after all. Er, sort of. At least it had been. Was she still welcome here now that they had Crissy back? Would Marc expect them to leave? Oh, hell. That was another whole set of problems that she wasn't ready to face.

"You look exhausted. I hope that doesn't mean something has happened with your sister?" The man frowned, worry clear in his gaze. "Is there is anything I can do?"

"Um. No. No, Crissy's sleeping, and both the kids have joined her. Rod's keeping an eye on them all. Madeline ordered me to come get a snack and go to bed." She shrugged and opened the fridge. "I don't think we managed to actually meet each other."

"True enough. It was rather a busy moment when Aldric whisked you out of that warehouse." The man smiled slightly, a twinkle lighting his gaze now that reminded her of Marc. He stood and faced her and bowed slightly. "I am Arthur Minton, Master of the Ulfred Coven and ally to the Frostwalker Clan. It was my honor to assist your people in clearing out that viper pit."

Faith blinked. A master vampire. Because of course a master vampire was sitting at the kitchen table at 4 am having what looked like chamomile tea and toast. A blob of jam practically gleamed on the crumb-covered plate next to his cup.

"Faith Latham. Um, freelance accountant," she said. "And I guess you know the rest." She bobbed her head, feeling very clumsy and tired and, well, *human*.

"Exhausted mage, worried sister, and beloved of Aldric Donnelly," Master Arthur nodded, a faint smile showing now. "I have heard a few things, yes. Why don't you sit and I'll make you something to eat? I don't think the toast was quite enough for me, either. Scrambled eggs sound good?"

He moved around the kitchen and somehow Faith found herself seated at the table with a cup of tea, watching the Master of the Ulfred Coven scramble eggs in sweatpants and bare feet.

"Thankfully it's not something I must worry about much anymore, but I remember another time when battles like that were far too common. It has always taken me a while to come down from the adrenaline. And you have the extra layer of relief at getting your sister back. I hear she will make a relatively quick recovery."

"Yeah, I suppose. It could have been a lot worse, I know, but seeing her so pale and weak..." Faith swallowed some tea and it burned on the way down. "I know she's safe now, but I didn't want to leave the room."

"I can definitely understand that," Master Arthur nodded, then grimaced. "I am frankly shocked by the scope of Conti's operation. He had managed to get far too organized without anyone noticing. I know that Marc is pretty disturbed as well. And the number of blighthounds penned in the caves behind the warehouse is more than a little terrifying."

He put a plate down in front of her, with toast slices neatly tucked under fluffy, golden eggs, then sat down with his plate.

Faith started to eat, and with the first bite realized how hungry she was. She hadn't eaten much more than a granola bar and a few cups of coffee since she got up the previous morning, and some soup when it was served to Crissy last night. When she finished her meal she glances up to find Master Arthur regarding her with some amuse-ment, but he didn't comment.

"Thanks," Faith muttered.

"It was no trouble at all," he answered. "I'm a little surprised that Aldric isn't here, fussing over you himself."

"I kinda threw him out of Crissy's room a while ago." Faith twisted her empty mug in careful circles. and couldn't bring herself to look up at the man. For a master vampire, he was shockingly easy to talk to. "He was hovering."

Master Arthur chuckled. "Yes, I imagine he was. I'm afraid he is likely to do more than a little hovering over you. It is in our nature to protect and care for those we bond with, but your young man has a great deal of hopeless romantic in him, I think, as well as the protector tendencies that make him such a good enforcer, so I suspect him to be even more prone to it."

Faith blinked at him. "We… um. We haven't done anything like that. The bonding, I mean."

Master Arthur nodded. "I have talked to him about the process a bit, yes, and Eldridge has as well I think. It seems that while Aldric's parents were themselves bonded, they never discussed much how it happens with him. While you have not completed a bond, it is true, there are threads already connecting you. It was how he found you so quickly once the attack started." Master Arthur tipped his head and smiled softly. "How we knew where to concentrate our forces in order to get to you in the shortest time. He cares for you very deeply."

"I know." She couldn't get her voice louder than a whisper. "I care for him, too."

Master Arthur's smile grew. "I am glad."

His smile turned into a grimace. "You will need allies, I am afraid. Conti and his people are dead, for the most part, but he is unlikely the only one who thinks the way he does. I promise you that the Ulfred Coven stands with you and the Frostwalker Clan, but none of us will be as dedicated to your safety as a bonded beloved."

"I thought that was just made-up romance novel language." Great. All the questions that spun wildly through Faith's mind and that was the one she managed to ask.

Master Arthur grinned now, his eyes dancing with laughter. "I'm trying to make it mainstream. I think it's a beautiful way to describe the relationship, don't you? The world could use more love and lightness, and it sounds way better than a *couple who are dedicated to each other through a magical bond between a vampire and their chosen significant other,* don't you think? That's just so clunky. And I appreciate the sentiment behind the word *mate* but it's just not as poetic, I think."

Faith blinked at him, then giggled. A second later she was laughing so hard tears gathered at the corners of her eyes and she was gasping for breath. Master Arthur looked pleased with himself and stood to collect the plates. When Faith finally caught her breath, he had washed the dishes and carefully stacked them in the dish drainer, and wiped down the counters.

"Feeling better?"

"I am, thanks," she said. Her whole body was heavy with exhaustion, but her heart felt lighter, finally. The terror of being kidnapped and the scope of Conti's plans had wrapped barbed wire bands around her chest that even their escape and safety in the clan house hadn't fully eased, but now she felt like she could take a breath.

Almost.

"I think you should go get that rest now. I'll finish closing down the kitchen and see if anyone else is still up aside from those on watch," Master Arthur said.

"On watch? But I thought it was over?" Faith frowned.

"Alpha Molin and his mutts weren't there. They had apparently left long before we arrived, though we're not sure why," Gregory grimaced again. "Marc and I both have trackers out and the Sun Ridge warriors are going out in the morning to search as well."

She had totally forgotten about Molin.

Well, he was a problem for another day. It was almost five in the morning, and she had a vampire to snuggle up with.

CHAPTER 21

Aldric sighed and rolled over again. He had woken to every sound all night. Every squeak of a floorboard as someone patrolled the house, every nocturnal creature outside that made noise in their hunts, every time a distant door closed, Aldric's eyes flew open, ready to defend his people.

He knew why, of course, but knowing a thing and doing something about it were often two entirely separate things. The only action Aldric could think to take that would settle his nerves enough to truly rest would be to go to Faith and drag her to bed. To make sure she was getting the rest she also needed but was no doubt denying herself at Crissy's bedside. And Aldric was not foolish enough of a barbarian as to try to separate the sisters now.

She would likely not thank him for the attempt. And in truth, Aldric could understand the need to stay close to her sister after so many weeks of worry and fear for Crissy's life. Aldric had deliberately not sought out her location in the house. He could, now that he was aware of the spider silk fine threads connecting them, but alone here, in the dark of his bedroom, he had to admit that he was afraid of what they meant.

Aldric rolled onto his back and adjusted his pillow. Glaring at the glowing red numbers on the clock for the hundredth time that night, he turned to glare instead at the ceiling. It was no more helpful but was rather less irritating than the reminder of how much sleep he wasn't getting.

What if now that her sister was safe and now that the main threat to her family had been eliminated, she wished to leave? To go back to her own life? It was a perfectly reasonable course of action, after all. But would she be willing to even stay in touch? Aldric and the others in the clan would, after all, be living reminders of a traumatic experience. He growled softly at the thought.

Footsteps in the hallway sounded like drumbeats in the quiet of the house. Someone walked with a light step, but in his hyper-alert state, they sounded loud and clear. Especially when they paused outside his door. He tensed and waited. The latch clicked and the door swung quietly open and Faith slipped in, chewing on her lip and peering at the bed.

She couldn't see that he was awake, he realized. His curtains were drawn and the room lay too dark for her human eyesight. She could probably only see vague shapes in the room.

"Faith?" he whispered.

She jerked, startled, but then her shoulders relaxed and she closed the door behind her.

"Everyone told me I should get some sleep in an actual bed," she answered, her voice hushed. "But I wondered... Um..."

Aldric waited for her to finish her thought, but when she went back to chewing on her lip, he sat up and reached a hand to her, not that she could see.

"Would you like to sleep in here? It can be difficult to be alone after a day like yesterday."

She nodded and hurried to his bed, stumbling slightly on the edge of his rug. When she got to him, she slid under the covers and settled against him, smelling of soap and toothpaste and somehow, of home. Aldric found himself pulling her close, and she curled into him, resting her head on his shoulder and sliding an arm over his waist.

"Thanks. Madeline and Crissy sorta threw me out of her room, and when I went to eat something, Master Arthur was having tea and toast and made us both some scrambled eggs. He seems nice."

Aldric nodded. "Indeed. I have only heard of him before yesterday, but his reputation is that of an honorable man and a fair coven master. I can also now confirm that he is an excellent fighter, as well."

"I'm glad. I think he wanted to reassure me that he wasn't going to go get flyers printed up that say 'Mages found in California!' or something, too,"

Aldric chuckled. "Indeed. He is nearly five hundred years old, I believe, and has been master of his coven since they moved to the U.S. some century and a half ago. I believe nearly the entire coven fought in World War Two in one capacity or another and saved many mages by hiding them."

Faith huffed a laugh and her breath blew across the skin of Aldric's shoulder, and he felt gooseflesh prickle down his arms. "I'm glad he came to help, then. Conti was crazy. I almost felt a little sorry for him and Cherro, though. Almost. I mean, it's not easy to watch someone you care about losing their grip on reality. Even if that person is a psychopathic war criminal who overdosed on eating people."

"You have a kind heart to be so generous to the people

who tried to use you."

"Don't get me wrong, Aldric. I was never more glad to see someone killed than I was when you swooped in like a superhero and smothered Conti. I have to admit that even though I'm not at all bloodthirsty, I felt nothing but relief when you ripped that man's heart out."

Aldric chuckled. "I think you can be forgiven for that sentiment."

"I didn't know that vampires could suffer from dementia?"

"I have heard of it in those who are very old. Ancient. If a vampire is unbonded, it is easier to slip away from the reality of so many centuries of memories," Aldric said. "Although Cherro was only a few hundred years old, Master Arthur suspects that the power he consumed from the mages he fed on overwhelmed his mind. Cherro's old master Wilhelm was said to be mad as a March hare in the documents describing his death. I suspect that was the great downfall of the whole coven. They went quite liter-ally mad with power."

"Conti seemed to think that drinking the blood of another powerful mage would reverse the dementia." Faith said. Aldric felt her shiver and ran his hand up and down her back, hoping to soothe the fear away.

"It would not have worked, and the question is moot. They will not threaten you again."

He felt her nod and curl closer to him.

"Um, something else Master Arthur said-- do you think he would be mad if I dropped his title? I'm not really into BDSM and it feels really strange to keep calling him Master. Anyhow," Faith kept going without letting Aldric answer one way or the other and he chuckled again and nodded. "Arthur also mentioned that you could find me at the warehouse because we've started bonding?"

Ah. Yes. Arthur and Uncle Eldridge both took him aside after they returned to discuss it. Crissy had fallen asleep almost immediately once they started the truck and headed back to the clan house, which they had decided was far easier to defend than the clinic in town, should it come to that. Faith was not going to leave her sister's side until Crissy was awake and whole again, so both of the older vampires had taken the opportunity to fill Aldric in about a great deal of the bonding process that his parents had neglected to educate him on.

"Yes," he said softly. He wasn't sure how she would take the information, but he would not start hiding things from her now. It wasn't who he was, and hiding information deliberately for whatever reason was one of the most annoying plot devices in the romance novels he enjoyed. "It seems that my parents neglected to inform me of large portions of the bonding process. We have begun very early bonding, yes. It is not irreversible at this stage, more like a confirmation of compatibility. I suspect it started when you fed me. Your magic and the magic that sustains my life meshed easily. Very easily, in fact, which is one reason I gained such a powerful ability so rapidly."

Aldric considered the information he had gained that evening from the other men, as well as their speculation on abilities. Conti's fireflies, as Faith called them, were impressive but overall not terribly powerful despite the skill with which he wielded them. The fact that even if two vampires fed from the same mage, they were not guaranteed to gain the same skills. Arthur speculated that the skill a vampire gains depends on several factors, one of which being compatibility.

It seemed a reasonable theory since through history it had been noticed that those vampires who befriended or fell in love with mages gained much stronger powers.

Those were the ones that wound up in popular mythology: turning to mist or into an animal or with the ability to influence a human mind. It is also where the common myths about a vampire's weakness comes from since it seemed that the more powerful the skill the greater the weakness.

Aldric felt he had gotten off easily. He was unlikely to enter a person's living space uninvited regardless of his being a vampire. It was simply poor manners.

"So ability depends on compatibility?" Faith asked. Her voice was sleepy and thoughtful.

"So it would seem. We cannot, of course, test the theory, but it feels plausible enough." Aldric glanced at the curtains where he could see the edges brightening as the sun rose.

"So we're really compatible?" she asked. "We started bonding?"

"Indeed," Aldric said. He wanted to say more but couldn't think how to even begin saying all that he wanted to express. "Nothing becomes permanent unless we choose to make it so, however. I am glad for even this small connection, though, since it led me straight to you yesterday afternoon. I cannot regret anything that helped me locate and rescue you and your sister."

"Mmmm," Faith hummed. "Me too."

A moment later, Aldric heard her breaths even out and her whole body softened with sleep. He lay awake still, staring at the ceiling again. This time, however, he felt nothing but contentment, and a determination to make certain that the woman in his arms felt safe enough to sleep well.

It was the least of what she deserved. And Aldric wanted to give it all to her.

CHAPTER 22

Faith woke up, warm and foggy and as comfortable as she could ever remember being. She pulled in a deep breath, getting ready to stretch and cozy memories of roasting marshmallows over campfires in the waning daylight, and of long, lazy chats over the dying coals, and of *comfort* and *home* flooded her mind inspired by the familiar scent embedded in the pillow, making her smile. When she managed to convince herself to roll over and open her eyes, the room was dim, but the bright sunshine peeking around the edges of the heavy blue curtains was plenty to see by.

On the bedside table, there was a travel mug, a bottle of painkillers, and a note, and she sat up to reach for both.

Faith,

As much as I would rather stay, I must go to perform my duties. I must arrange for the ceremonies in the Enforcer's Grove for those we lost in the battle. I stopped to speak with Crissy to assure her of your location, but she and Rod were deep in conversation, so I did not linger. The children are with Marc and Greg in the schoolroom.

The coffee was very hot when I left it, so I hope it is still warm enough to drink. I was uncertain if you would need them, but I have left some painkillers as well, in case.

Good morning,

Aldric

Faith grinned as she took a cautious sip of coffee, finding it a perfect temperature. She peered around the room until she found the small analog clock that Aldric had set on his dresser. Ten twenty… something. She was too sleepy still and the room was too dark to make it out exactly, but it was close enough. Only around four hours of sleep.

Still, she grinned to herself. Faith wasn't sure how she'd gotten it into her head to try to sneak into Aldric's bed this morning, but she was glad she had. His presence soothed her and drove away the shadows of Conti and his creeps, and of the fate she had narrowly avoided.

She knew she was free because of Aldric and Marc and the others who attacked the warehouse, and she had to thank them, but just now, while she sat in Aldric's bed, drinking coffee he had left her and taking the medicine that he had thoughtfully provided as well— because she did ache absolutely everywhere— Faith just smiled. She was safe and she knew it to her bones.

When the coffee was gone, she swung her legs over the edge of the bed and stood, stretched, and shuffled into the hallway. She smiled when she got to the door of her room as she heard Kaylee squeal in the new classroom down the hall. The squeal turned into a laugh, Jake's laughter a happy counterpoint. Greg was chuckling, too, and making noises that sounded like they were trying to get the kids back on task.

She wished him luck.

After she got dressed, she peeked in on Crissy, who was

asleep. Rod looked up from the book he was reading and nodded a greeting. Faith smiled and nodded back.

"Aldric is in his office," he said, his voice just above a whisper. "Crissy just dozed off a few minutes ago."

"I'll go find him then. Thanks for keeping her company."

"My pleasure," Rod answered. If Faith didn't know better, she would swear that his ears turned red. She cocked an eyebrow at him and he shrugged. Faith chuckled softly as she headed to Aldric's office. That could be interesting.

She heard voices as she neared Aldric's office door.

"...just don't understand why you're in here and not upstairs with Faith, that's all. You were frantic yesterday," Marc said.

"She needed rest, Marc. And no doubt she needs more time with her family. I will not begrudge her that," Aldric answered. "Besides, this needs to be done. We lost three sentries yesterday and they deserve all the honor we can give them."

Marc sighed. "That is true. But I could arrange the ceremonies just as easily. And you *are* Faith's family. You get to spend time with her, too. And you should probably get to know her sister, as well."

"He's right, you know," Faith stepped into the room and went straight to Aldric's desk, to lean over and peck a kiss on his upturned face. "You are family. So are you, Marc. And Jake and Tamika and, well..." Faith shrugged and perched on the arm of Aldric's chair for a moment before he wrapped an arm around her waist and pulled her into his lap.

Marc laughed. "Thank you, Faith."

A knock on the door stopped whatever he was about to say. They looked over when Tamika stepped in.

"The Council reps are finally here." Her tone left no question as to her opinion on that.

"Might as well send them in here," Marc sighed.

A few minutes later, three large men walked in, glancing between Aldric and Marc.

"Gentlemen," Marc stood. "Marc Keller, Chief of the Frostwalker Clan." He held his hand out and they all shook politely. "That is Aldric Donnelly, our Chief Enforcer, and his beloved, Faith Latham."

"Pleasure to meet you all," the man in front nodded. "Dwayne Linsby. I was told you have some problems. An aggressive wolf pack and some rogue vampires?"

Faith snorted, drawing attention. Dwayne cocked an eyebrow at her, very clearly communicating his disbelief that she had any place in this conversation.

Faith's patience suddenly snapped. She was in here trying to have a nice moment when these arrogant nitwits roll in here like they had the first clue about anything?

"Oh, I am not getting dismissed with an eyebrow. First off, it took you all how goddamn long to show up? My sister was being held by those psychopaths for weeks! *Weeks!* They threatened me and my niece, who is *five*, and attacked not only us but innocent people out in the community. They were stockpiling weapons, kidnapping anyone they felt like, and running emergency vehicles off the road! In broad daylight! Then when they kidnapped me, too, you didn't think that was worthy of lighting a fire under your asses to get here to help?"

Faith stood up and glared at the wolf in front of her, stabbing her finger at Dwayne to make her point. "Then you saunter your lazy, arrogant asses in here and minimize our problems as *an aggressive wolf pack and some rogue vampires?* You jackass. The Frostwalkers and our allies stopped World War Three yesterday when they took out Conti and

Cherro and their actual goddamn *army* and you stand there with a sneer, talking about *rogue vampires?* Screw you and your pathetic excuse for a 'Council.' These two said you have a court that's worth more than ten cents? I sure as hell hope so. Take our prisoners and get the hell out of here you sad excuse for a lapdog."

The Council wolves' eyes grew huge as she snarled at them, and by the time she was done, one of them stepped up, white as a sheet.

"Um, did you say Cherro? As in Reyher Cherro?" he asked.

"She did, in fact. And Sandalio Conti and the rest of the leftovers from the Immortal Thirst Coven. Did you not read the report I sent? They were amassing weapons and like-minded young idiots in a nearby warehouse. And they had a fairly large pack of blighthounds, as well," Marc confirmed drily. He had resumed his seat while Faith was yelling at them and beamed at her. "And I wouldn't make her too angry if I was you. It tends to be unhealthy. She doesn't look like much, but she can and will kick your ass."

Faith smirked now. Aldric's hand came up to rest on her hip.

"Faith has saved my life on several occasions. Discount her at your own peril."

"I'm sorry, I'm still back on Cherro and Conti. And you were kidnapped by them? Why? And how did you get away? We have to call our supervisor and figure out some way to stop them." Dwayne was pulling out his phone as he spoke.

Faith laughed. "Were you not listening? We *already* stopped them. Well, mostly Aldric, Marc, and the rest of them did. I was busy protecting my sister and getting the hell out of there. We had some help from some nearby allies, but not a damn thing from this supposed *'Council'* that you think is so useful." She used heavily sarcastic air quotes around 'Council' again, and Marc brought his hand up to cover his grin.

Dwayne blinked. "The Frostwalker Clan, a small-town clan of mostly werewolves, took out a vampire war criminal and one of the most dangerous young coven leaders we've heard of? We've been collecting rumors about Conti for years, trying to get evidence we could use to bring charges, but nobody would testify."

"Well, it's a moot point now. He's about as dead as a vampire can get. Aldric ripped his heart straight out of his chest and dropped it on what was left of his corpse once it shriveled up."

"And I would do it again, but more slowly," Aldric growled behind her. She glanced down and saw the red bleeding into his eyes.

There was some uncomfortable shifting and mutters from the Council wolves. Dwayne turned back to murmur something to his team, then turned back to Aldric.

"We're going to need a full report," he said. "And I think we need to see this warehouse."

"We'll be happy to tell you what happened. Not that it matters, mind you. The Council has nearly no jurisdiction over this sort of thing, and even if it did, they wouldn't do anything about it," Marc said. He sat back in his chair and raised an eyebrow. "Finding evidence is well and good, but only useful to a court."

Faith settled back down on Aldric's lap and noticed that neither of the men had offered seats to Dwayne or his men. Politics was very odd.

"And why would they want you, miss?" Dwayne turned back to Faith, nervously glancing at Aldric as he continued. "No disrespect intended at all, but it seems curious that a group of vampires bent on ruling over the human race as if they were gods, would be so interested in a single human. Or a pair of human sisters."

Marc shrugged at her, leaving the decision up to Faith. Tell these wolves her secret-- not that it was incredibly secret anymore anyway-- or let them draw their own conclusions.

"Why do you care?" she asked after a moment. "Would you try to take me away somewhere if we told you? Would you post guards around the Frostwalker territory? Would you try to take over the clan or something? What would you and your Council do with the knowledge?"

Dwayne's shoulders sagged a bit and an exhausted expression crept over his face as she spoke.

"May I sit?" He gestured at the chair beside Marc and Aldric nodded. Dwayne dropped into the seat and grimaced.

"There are a number of us trying to change things. When the Council was set up, it was meant to prevent people like Conti and Cherro from ever doing something like this again, but everyone was so afraid of a group of paranormals gaining any sort of power at that point that they defanged the administrative arm before it even got finished forming." Dwayne glanced up at Marc, then at Aldric. "I had hoped to discuss it with you, Chief Keller, before we left with the prisoners you asked us to take to the judicial complex. We want to form an Enforcers arm of the Council. A paranormal police force, if you will. People that can go out and investigate rumors like the ones we'd heard about Conti and step in where needed rather than relying on each pack, coven, or clan investigating and apprehending suspects themselves and then essentially using the Council Courts as a holding system."

"But?" Marc raised a brow at him.

Dwayne shrugged. "You know how politics can go.

Half the Council wants to use it to enforce their own ideals and personal agendas, and the other half is enthusiastic about the concept but can't agree on any details whatsoever. Most of the Council members are so old and hidebound that they can't see progress when it hits them in the face. Most of them don't even own computers, for crying out loud. I was hoping I could convince you to run for a Council seat in the next cycle." He looked up at Marc. "I've heard of you. People who pass through here all comment on how peaceful it is, and how welcome they felt when they came to let you know they were in your territory. Any leader who can hold a territory like this for this long without any negative comments being circulated is likely to be a good, strong leader. I hoped I'd get here and see for myself, and if I was right, talk you into running."

Faith felt her jaw drop. That was not at all what she'd expected to hear. From the look on Marc's face, it wasn't what he'd expected either.

"I..." Marc shook his head slowly. "I am going to need to think about this. We'll talk about it more after you see the warehouse. For now--"

Marc broke off at the sound of howling and snarls from the back of the house. Everyone looked out the window but saw nothing but the edge of the lawn and the trees from this vantage.

"Faith, stay here." Aldric lifted her easily as he stood and placed her gently on the chair.

"Like hell!" she said to thin air since he had already run out the door.

"Miss, really, whatever is going on out there isn't a safe thing for a human," Dwayne said, as he turned to follow Aldric and Marc.

"Good goddamn thing I'm not just human, then, isn't it?" she snarled back at him and dashed after the others.

She got to the door leading out to the deck just in time to see Marc in his wolf form leaping at another large wolf who was snarling and growling and almost bigger than Marc was.

It seemed that they weren't going to have to keep searching for the remaining Goldfang Stalkers after all.

CHAPTER 23

Aldric slammed out the door onto the deck and swore. The entire clearing was full of werewolves in both forms fighting and snarling. Marc was facing off against a huge grey and tawny wolf that could only be Alpha Molin. The alphas were closely flanked by Ori and Kenya in their wolf forms facing off against two others Aldric didn't know, likely Molin's enforcers.

To his left, Eldridge, Lucy, and Greg had formed a line between a group of Goldfangs and the kids near the playset, Jake in his wolf form again baring his tiny puppy teeth in a surprisingly fierce snarl was held in Kaylee's arms. Even as he glanced at them, Aldric saw Greg Honeyford force one of the Goldfang bruisers back with a very tidy palm strike to the guy's nose. Aldric was reassured to know that he was no helpless victim, even if he wasn't a fighter at heart. Lucy took another down with a series of moves Aldric knew he would be begging her to teach his Enforcers after this was settled.

To his immediate right, Rod was standing firm

between three Goldfangs and Crissy, who was backed up against the wall. Her eyes were wide and unfocused and darted around the clearing from wolf to wolf, but every time Rod barked something at her, she answered. Tamika was close by, tearing into a group that was trying to get to where Rod defended the older Latham sister.

Past them, several Sun Ridge wolves and a few of the Ulric Coven vampires very effectively took out more Goldfangs, leaving bleeding wolves in their wake. Master Arthur snarled at a wolf who was foolish enough to try to leap on his back. All this was noted in the few seconds before he felt a large presence behind him.

"Good lord. This is what you've been dealing with?" Dwayne muttered behind him.

"Welcome to our summer," Aldric snarled back and stepped forward to help Rod.

"No," Faith's voice stopped him in his tracks. "Not again, *fuck* no. I have goddamn *had it* with these assholes!"

"Faith," he started to say, but she stalked past him and down the steps headed straight for Marc and Molin, every movement full of fury and determination.

Aldric had little choice and fell in right behind her, hissing at any wolf who turned their way. He was not about to let her wander through a battlefield unprotected. Several of his sentries joined them as they crossed the grass to the center of the fight where the two leaders snapped and clawed at each other. Molin was a slimy, unscrupulous jerk, but as it turned out, he was also a strong fighter.

When they reached some point that satisfied her, Faith reached her arm back like she was getting ready to pitch a baseball and the biggest fireball Aldric had seen yet flew straight at the Goldfang Alpha, hitting him in the shoulder just before he leaped at Marc, and splattered flames down the wolf's entire side. Molin yelped in shock and pain, loud enough to draw the attention of the fighters nearby who turned to see what happened.

Molin dropped to the grass and rolled, trying to smother his burning fur and Marc limped back toward where Faith stood tall and furious. He was bleeding from several wounds and the fur on his right foreleg was matted with blood, but he stood tall as he flanked Faith on her other side.

"You unbelievably slimy, arrogant, *mangy* jackass!" Faith was muttering, though every wolf around could hear her clearly. The battle was dying slowly, as more of the fighters noticed the confrontation in the middle of the clearing. "How dare you even *consider* attacking us again? You and those dipshit vampires at that stupid warehouse. I have goddamn had *enough* of this bullshit!"

Faith reached out her hand and spread her fingers, and Aldric could sense the power she was trying to draw. He reached out and lay a hand on her shoulder, silently offering whatever he could, and after a moment he felt her power brush against his. Their magic had already touched once, forming the spider silk bonds between them. Now it blended easily as if the magic that sustained Aldric had simply been waiting for the chance to power Faith, as well.

"Who do you assholes think you are, coming in here, attacking us, trying to kidnap people as if we were toys you didn't want to share!" Faith snarled, scooping her hand up into the air. Molin yelped again, the fear and shock clear in the sound, as he rose off the grass and into the air. The big wolf flailed, trying to gain purchase on some sort of surface but Faith was relentless and the air gave Molin nowhere to plant his paws.

Marc leaned his shoulder into her hip on her other side in more silent support and Faith used her free hand to dig her fingers into the fur of his back. Aldric wondered idly if she was drawing power from him, as well. Marc could lend her magic as her Alpha— her Chief— and Aldric idly thought it was interesting that he felt no jealousy over that idea.

"Call. Off. Your. Mutts." Faith snarled. "And I will consider letting you down gently. Otherwise, we all get to find out if wolves land on their feet like cats do." She raised her hand again and Molin rose perhaps fifteen feet into the air over their heads.

He whined and his legs scrabbled uselessly through the air. He didn't need to tell his pack to stand down as the whole field had grown silent, but Faith growled again in a shockingly wolf-like manner, and Molin tipped his head back to howl the Goldfang's loss.

"Was that good enough, Chief? Shall I let him down?" Faith didn't turn to look at Marc when she asked, and Marc didn't look back at her when he huffed his affirmative, then barked an order to the Frostwalkers surrounding them.

"Frostwalkers!" Aldric raised his voice to make sure the order was heard by all. "Take the Goldfangs into custody! Chief Keller will decide what to do with them shortly!"

"And you Goldfangs had better goddamn go nicely or you will regret every one of your life choices!" Dwayne hollered from behind them. "We are here on behalf of the Paranormal Council and the Frostwalker Clan is well within its rights to press charges against every wolf here that chose to take part in this attack! I promise, if they don't simply turn you over to us, whatever fate these three come up with will be nicer than what you'll find in our prison." Aldric could hear the satisfied grin in the man's last words.

"You can let him down, now, beloved," Aldric leaned in

to murmur in her ear. A shiver raced through her shoulder where his hand rested, humming with their connection.

"Flirting in the middle of a fight?" Her words were fond, but Aldric could hear the strain in her voice. "Fine. I guess I'll let him down."

She slowly lowered the whimpering wolf, his fur on one side charred and still smoking slightly, and he was immediately surrounded by Kenya and Ori and two large wolves Aldric didn't recognize, but who looked to Dwayne for orders. He stepped past Aldric to nod at his men.

"Stay and guard Molin, for now, to free up the Frost-walkers. There's enough of these jerks that it will take all of us to process them. I'll call for more transports in a short while after I've talked to Chief Keller," Dwayne said, and with their nods, he turned to the three of them, nodded to Marc and Aldric, then bowed to Faith. Aldric expected him to immediately want to know about Faith's magic, but the man surprised them.

"Beloved?" he smirked. "I thought that was only something in those ridiculous romance novels the humans write about vampires?"

"We're trying to bring it into fashion in real life. Sounds much better than anything else we've come up with," Faith grinned. Aldric slid his hand across her back and around her other shoulder, letting her lean into him. He could feel her exhaustion in every bit of her skin that he touched.

"I plan to encourage it with my own people when we get back home," Master Arthur said, striding up to them, still fully vampire. "Chief Keller, my people will assist yours with the cleanup. Red asked me to convey the same for his wolves. Enforcer Rod tells me that you do not have enough space in your cells for all these mutts, so we felt that perhaps small groups could be confined to the remaining guestrooms. He and I can organize that while you attend to the injured and retrieve clothing if that is acceptable to you?"

Marc nodded once and yipped his confirmation.

"Excellent. Magaestra, if you will allow some advice?" Master Arthur waited for her to nod. "My mother always made sure she had a large meal after any major magic use. Something hearty and filling may help you recover some of your energy." He flicked a glance to Aldric, telling him that Aldric would likely benefit from something similar, then winked at him.

"Thanks, Master Arthur. That sounds like a great idea."

"Just Arthur, please. My friends don't need to be so formal." He met Aldric's gaze again, then looked to Marc, to make sure they knew they were included, then turned and hurried over to where Rod was directing the cleanup while holding Crissy close to his side. Interestingly, she clung to the large man with one hand and clutched Kaylee to her side with the other. Greg, Lucy, Eldridge, and Jake all hovered close to the trio.

"Shall we go inside and arrange for food for everyone? I suspect it is not only you who would benefit from a meal." Aldric rubbed his hand up and down her arm and when she leaned more of her weight into him, he smiled softly.

"Yeah. Let's call out for pizza or something, and then you and I can have snacks while we wait." Faith glanced over to Crissy who had moved to kneel with Kaylee and fussed over Jake, who squirmed and tumbled like the excited puppy he was. Lucy glanced over at them and winked. "I guess Crissy and the kids will be in soon, too. Juice boxes and snacks. And maybe we put the boots away until Jake is a boy again."

Aldric laughed his agreement and helped Faith back to the house.

It was good to know that their enemies were all stopped cold at last. At least for now.

CHAPTER 24

" $\mathbf{S}$ o this is our life now?"

Crissy slumped back into the mountain of pillows on her bed and picked at a wrinkle in the quilt that lay over her legs. Faith raised a brow at her sister.

"Cozy quilts and hot guys doting on us? How awful." After Faith had eaten three sandwiches and had a very large cup of coffee, she had followed Rod, who carried Crissy through the kitchen and up to her room to tuck her in carefully before bringing her a tray piled with snacks. Greg had been right behind them, ushering the kids up to the classroom while most of the adults helped with cleanup outside.

Aldric had made sure that several pizzas had been brought up to the five of them when they were delivered, and that they had all the drinks they wanted, and Rod stopped in shortly after Aldric left to make sure they didn't need anything.

Faith was very amused at the huge, bald man blushing when Crissy thanked him for his thoughtfulness.

Crissy smirked at her for a moment. "You know that's

not what I mean." Her expression turned pensive again. "And they all know now. They all know about our magic."

Faith sighed. "Aldric has known from the very start. He found me and Kaylee trapped behind my shield, remember? Marc has known almost as long, and we told the inner circle of Enforcers before we tried to rescue you the first time."

"But..." Crissy grimaced and glanced at the door. "But you've been attacked again since then. And the kids. Rod told me that Jake shouldn't be able to shift yet."

Faith nodded. Jake was at least ten years early for running on four paws.

"Yeah. And Kaylee has some pretty bad nightmares. She has her own room but ends up in someone's bed more often than not. Mine, Jake's. I even found her curled up with Aldric once, while he sat up and read. Has he lent you any books yet?" Faith grinned suddenly.

"Um, no? I'm not sure I want to read anything a vampire enjoys." Crissy shivered. "I mean, he seems nice and Kaylee has gushed about him, but I'm sorry Faith. I can't." The shivers grew and Crissy wrapped her arms around herself.

Faith moved over to sit on the bed and wrap her arms around her big sister. "I know. You have every reason to be traumatized. God, I'm sorry it took us so long to find you."

"You can't let him bite you, Faith. You don't even know how awful it is." Crissy's voice was broken, and she spoke into Faith's shoulder, her words muffled.

Faith sighed. She really couldn't hide this, especially considering how traumatized her sister had been. Something that Faith remembered as a pleasant, intimate experience was for her sister a violent, horrifying memory.

"He has bitten me, Cris."

Crissy's head snapped up. "What? No! You said he was a *good guy!* You promised me, Faith!"

"He is a good guy. I *made* him do it. You remember I told you that when we rescued Greg and searched the Goldfang's camp for you, Aldric and I got trapped in a cave for a bit?"

Crissy nodded. "That's when he attacked you?"

"No. That's when he was crushed by a boulder and almost died in the freezing cold darkness under the damn mountain." Faith shivered herself now, hating the memory of Aldric's weak voice telling her not to feed him. "I knew that if he got some fresh blood he could start to heal, and I was already bleeding from the fall and he *still* didn't want to drink, the stubborn jerk. That's how he could turn into a mist-like that at the warehouse. That's from my magic."

Crissy shivered again. "Conti went on about that. About how he was going to give my power to his army. About how he was going to catch you and some guy and restore Cherro to full health or something. What did he mean by that, do you know?"

Crissy was distracted now by her memories. Faith wasn't sure that was a good thing or a bad one and made a note to ask Marc about therapists who knew about the paranormal.

Faith huffed a laugh and sat back. "Apparently, Conti was under the odd impression that even though too much magic drove Cherro to dementia, the cure for that was feeding him more power." Faith rolled his eyes. "I don't think that's how it works, do you?"

Crissy wrinkled her forehead and shrugged. "I have no idea."

"Anyhow, Aldric didn't want to drink from me for a lot of reasons, one of them being that he swore to the old chief that he would never drink from a human again when he joined the Frostwalkers. Turns out he didn't really understand the whole point of it all, and Marc had to explain that life-threatening circumstances and, uh, very intimate moments were implicitly excluded from that agreement." She cleared her voice and knew she was blushing.

Crissy's eyes went wide. "Oh my god, you sounded just like him! All stiff and formal."

That did not help the heat in Faith's face. Crissy laughed.

"And you should see your face! You're redder than Rudolph's nose!" Crissy snorted and clapped a hand over her mouth, which only made her laugh harder. After a few minutes, Faith started chuckling, too.

"What? I like hanging out with him. And you will too, once you're more comfortable. I'll bring some of his books. They're full of rugged heroes and plucky heroines and adventure and some of them have scenes that make *him* blush. He's adorkable and has a romance novel collection you're going to be so jealous of."

Crissy lay back on the pillows, her jaw on her chest and her eyes wide with shock. "He reads romance novels?"

"Yep," Faith smirked. "*Paranormal* romance novels. About vampires and werewolves and so on."

Crissy couldn't possibly make her eyes any larger. "Get out."

"Cross my heart." Faith grinned. Her eyes slid towards the door. "I'll go pick out some good wolf shifter books for you."

It was Crissy's turn to blush now.

"God it's so good to have you back." Faith leaned forward and hugged her sister again. "I know it wasn't that long. Just a few weeks, but it felt like forever."

"For me, too." Crissy agreed. "That dipshit Honeyford

wasn't so bad. I still can't believe that total sweetheart Greg is Jesse's brother! Oh shit, He's Kaylee's uncle!"

"Yep. She even started calling him Uncle Greg and he cried the first time. It seems that the only person Jesse cares about is his little brother. Turned on Molin so fast we all saw spots when we told the guy about Molin kidnapping Greg, and when Greg went down there and lit into him Jesse practically begged for a chance to tell us everything he could think of. Anyhow, don't change the subject. Well, okay, I guess you can, but first I'm just going to say that Rod is a great guy and I approve. Especially if he makes you blush like that. I have *never* seen you blush like that."

Crissy sighed and turned to stare out the window. Evening was falling now, and the sounds of the cleanup had started to fade. Nobody had died today, thank any deity that was listening-- Faith was starting to wonder if they all did and maybe she'd be meeting some soon, with the way her life had been going. The silence stretched for a while and settled around the sisters as they both got lost in their own thoughts.

"I suppose I've been fired by now, huh? I only asked for a week off," Crissy said.

"I talked to your boss, actually. Told her that you'd been kidnapped and the police were searching," Faith said. "You should call her, she was really upset to hear it."

"And what are we going to tell the cops? That we raided a nest of vampires bent on world domination?" Crissy sounded bitter and Faith couldn't blame her. "They'll lock us up in a nuthouse and lose the key."

"First, we'll tell them that our private investigator found you, and learned that a Federal raid was going to take place, so he sent them his file on you and when you were rescued and debriefed, you were sent home to recover,"

Faith said. She knew she was smirking at Crissy as her sister's eyebrows rose.

"That was a very quick answer."

"Yep. Marc and Aldric and I talked about it before I got snatched. We discussed it with Ken, too, and this was the cover story we came up with," Faith said. "Once the cops got involved, we knew we would need something to tell them if we had to rescue you ourselves. Which honestly seemed likely."

Crissy nodded and turned back to the window. After a minute she said, "You said that was first. What's second?"

"Second is that even if the cops do want us to answer questions or whatever, you could be shielded by Madeline as your doctor, and then on top of that, Marc has a lawyer ready and waiting. A clan member who knows almost everything and is ready to come to our defense if necessary. So don't stress out about that part, okay?"

Crissy nodded but didn't turn back from the window.

Faith reached out to take Crissy's hand. "I'm pretty sure that there are also a few therapists in the clan. You could talk to them and not have to hide anything."

Crissy nodded slowly. "Sounds like I would have to stay here to see them, though."

Faith shrugged slightly and squeezed Crissy's hand. "It's a nice place to live. You'll like Tamika. And Marc. He makes an amazing venison pot roast."

Crissy's eyebrows rose and she turned back to Faith at that. "Venison pot roast?"

"Yep." Faith grinned. "And of course, Rod's here. And Jake. You wouldn't want to separate the two musketeers. We'd never hear the end of the whining— human AND puppy! Oh, Kaylee is desperate to be a shifter, she says. Like Jake and Uncle Greg. No mention of Jesse whatsoever."

Crissy snorted. "I suppose I can allow that. Greg was pretty awesome before all this, even if he did accidentally start all the trouble."

"He still is pretty awesome. I don't know if you saw, but he was kicking some furry butt this morning. Aunt Lucy, too. I think Aldric wants her to teach some classes for his security people."

"The scary, badass vampire wants an old human lady to teach his werewolf army about self-defense techniques?" Crissy blinked several times, clearly trying to picture it.

"The intelligent leader of security and not-very-secret romance novel reader sees an excellent opportunity to expand his people's skillset. And I think he wants to give her an excuse to stick around. She and Uncle Eldridge have been pretty cozy since she got here."

"Good lord," Crissy clapped her free hand over her eyes and slumped back. "These Frostwalker men have a fetish for our family."

Faith snorted. "Oh my god, Crissy!"

"Well!" Crissy sat up and poked Faith in the arm. "You've got Aldric panting after you. Aunt Lucy is apparently being drooled over by this Eldridge guy, wait. Whose uncle is he? Marc's?"

"Aldric's. He's Madeline and Leo's father. You haven't met Leo yet, but he's been hacking like a lunatic the last few days to find you. I think he's asleep now, finally."

"So," Crissy paused, chewing her lip for a minute. "So Eldridge, Madeline, and Leo are all vampires, too?"

"Yep. They're the good guys, Cris."

Crissy frowned but nodded slowly. "And Kaylee even has Jake wrapped around her little finger I've noticed," she said, not commenting on the short diversion.

"And you have Rod blushing. I think he's going to get teased a bit for that, I doubt blushing is something he's known for around here. Being super grumpy before coffee, yes. Being adorably lovesick? Not so much," Faith laughed.

"Coffee, huh? Good to know. You two have that in common."

Faith smacked her sister's shoulder.

They sat there, grinning at each other for a long moment.

"Sounds like I'm going to have to call my boss and let her know I'm moving, huh?" Crissy said with a shrug. "Madeline was grumbling about not having enough hands to deal with the wounded here *and* work at the clinic. Guess I could offer to help out once she lets me do stuff again."

Faith wasn't sure she could smile any wider.

CHAPTER 25

Aldric stood from his desk chair and stretched his arms as far to the ceiling as he could before twisting left and right, causing more popping from his spine than he liked to hear. After an exhausting day of finally ending the conflict with the Goldfangs, caring for Faith, Crissy, and the children, assisting the Council team in recording the names of all the prisoners and organizing their transport, and watching Marc take charge of everyone there, including the Sun Ridge wolves and the Ulfred Coven vampires *and* the Council team much to the impressed chagrin of Dwayne Linsby, Aldric was more than ready to at last get some dinner.

"You look completely done."

Aldric blinked and turned to see Faith leaning on the door frame, a small smile on her lips, and two cups of coffee in her hand.

"I am, fortunately, finished for the evening. I hope." With one last stretch, he dropped his arms and stepped away from his desk.

"Don't stop on my account. I was enjoying the show," she said.

Aldric raised an eyebrow at the gleam in her gaze. She didn't elaborate but held the coffee out to him. He took a sip and raised both his brows this time.

"There is blood in this?"

Faith shrugged and moved to sit on the sofa. "I guessed that you might need a little extra something after this week. What with the rescue yesterday, then the battle this morning, and all the stress and nonsense from everything that's been going on you're bound to be a bit worn out. Marc pulled some meat out of the fridge to make stew a bit ago and I asked him to pour off the meat juice into a pitcher for some fancy vampire coffee. Arthur's men all started texting people back at their coven, and Arthur said it reminded him of his mother's coffee and got all nostalgic. I can't imagine why it isn't more of a thing."

Aldric smiled. "I believe it is an old-fashioned idea. I remember my father doing something similar when I was a child." He sipped at the coffee and sighed, the caffeine and the blood working their wonders on his body. When he had taken another sip he looked over at Faith. She had the air of someone settled, of someone that had made a plan and was ready to see it through, and Aldric prayed to any deity that might listen to him that she included him in her plan.

Faith grinned. "Well, I think it's smart. I'm bringing it back."

Aldric took a step then stopped and looked at her for a moment as she sipped her coffee. "I certainly would not be upset. And I suspect that Madeline and Leo would both enjoy the idea of their coffee laced with blood as a more publicly consumable manner of sustaining themselves while they work." He took the last few steps and sank onto the sofa next to her. "How is your sister?"

Faith's grin faded. "She's going to need a lot of therapy, I think. But I think she'll be okay." She took a deep breath and let it out slowly, pondering her next words. "I think, mostly, she doesn't feel safe. Anywhere. Although, when either Aunt Lucy or, surprisingly, Rod is around, she seems less tense. She probably thinks she's hiding it well, but I can see it. Aunt Lucy can, too. Marc has given me a list of therapists in the clan, and I told Crissy I have it. When she's ready, we'll get her the help she needs. Right now, though, I think she needs to see the proof that she's safe."

"This morning likely did not help," Aldric grimaced. "I could swear to her that we will be dedicated to her security, and that of you and Kaylee and Lucy as well, but words are simple to utter and mean very little to someone in this situation."

Faith grinned. "You got all stiff again."

Aldric shrugged and sipped his coffee.

"Oh, don't hide. I like it," She said. She shifted to lean her head on his shoulder, snuggling herself close to him, and he took the hint, wrapping his arm around her shoulders. Faith relaxed and sighed in what Aldric hoped was contentment.

"So, I talked to Crissy. Ugh, I think I've talked to everyone in the house today. Dwayne swore that the Council won't do anything when they find out about me. I don't really believe that, but I think he does," Faith sighed. "But, that's a problem for another day. I know that he was talking to Marc about joining the Council or something, so there's a lot of politics about to happen."

"That is true. There have always been those who wished to use mages for their own ends. They do not know about any other mages to bother, at least. And Kaylee still scents as a wolf, so it is, unfortunately, you, Crissy, and

Detective Lincoln that will be primarily caught up in this Council nonsense, whatever it is that happens."

Aldric wished he could somehow manage time, or perhaps that he had the mythological vampires' ability to cloud minds and erase memories so that he could protect Faith and her family. But there was nothing he could do in this case but be prepared to defend them if necessary. And he did not doubt that it could become very necessary. Would he have to send sentries and bodyguards with them if they moved back to the city?

"I suppose that everything will be very complicated for a while, won't it?" Faith asked.

"I am afraid that is likely, yes." Aldric balanced his coffee mug on his knee. He had to know what her plans were. The uncertainty was eating away at his concentration. "You have decided on a course of action. May I inquire about it?"

She laughed softly. "I don't know how you make stiff and formal sound so damn adorable," she murmured into his shoulder before sitting up to look him in the eye. "We, that is, Crissy and I, are very concerned about our security going forward."

"I can arrange security for you both. All three of you. I would never leave Miss Kaylee unguarded," Aldric said.

Faith's lips twitched as if she was trying not to smile again.

"Indeed," she said. There was a smile in her voice at least, and Aldric wondered what she was amused at. Likely him, somehow.

"I am missing something," he said, sure of it.

"You are. A little bit of implied information, but I intended to make myself clear momentarily," Faith said.

Aldric blinked. "And now you are making fun of me."

"Only a little. Crissy noticed that I've picked up a few

of your speech patterns." Faith did smile now. "I don't mind, really. Makes me feel like you're with me, even when you're not."

Aldric had no idea what to say to that.

"I will put you out of your confused misery," Faith said. She turned to look him fully in the eye, and a small smile danced on her face. "Crissy and I plan to stay here. To move here permanently." Faith tipped her head in question. "Not that we're sure where we will live or any of that, but I was hoping that at least Crissy and Kaylee could stay here in the clan house for a while. Until she feels safer in the world."

"Of course. They are Frostwalkers. You are all members of the Frostwalker Clan, you may stay here as long as you wish to." Aldric. reached out and put his mug on the table beside the sofa. He was sure that he would drop it soon if this conversation continued much longer.

"Then we'll need to go pack up my apartment and their house. And Greg's as well," Faith said. "And..." now she glanced away, pulling her lower lip between her teeth and worrying at it.

Aldric had his hand up, his thumb easing her lip out from between her teeth before he even consciously thought about it. "And?"

"And I suppose we should make a decision about this bonding thing. I..." Faith took a deep breath and her expression was soft, though also serious. "I think it sounds nice. We've already started bonding, you said. How does that work? I know they're fiction, but you said that some of the things in your books are close to the truth."

"It is not like in the books. It is not a simple matter of sex and a bite and now a couple is permanently bound forever." That would be far too simple and easy to do in the heat of passion. Far too easy to spend eternity regretting it and unable to anything about it.

"I didn't think it would be that easy," Faith sighed. "Tell me what it does involve then."

Aldric wondered if it was possible for a heart to actually beat right out of a person's chest. His certainly seemed to be attempting it.

"Mostly," Aldric's voice cracked and he reached for his mug to drain the last swallow from it and then tried again. "Um.

"Mostly it involves being close for some time. The foundation of the bond will grow naturally. We accelerated the process when you fed me. Being intimate would result in a similar acceleration if that is something you are interested in."

Faith's lips twitched. "Accelerating the bond or being intimate?"

Aldric felt very warm. "Er. Both."

Faith nodded thoughtfully, though the mirth was still there in her expression. "And how do we finish it, then?"

"There is a spell we recite together, and then yes, we do exchange blood as it is the fastest way to share our magics. It would be easiest for me to bite you, or," Aldric glanced at the empty coffee mug. "Perhaps we could make coffee."

Faith laughed at that, then tipped her head. "Share our magic, hmm? So vampires never bond with humans?"

Aldric shrugged. "Every living thing has at least a little magic. It is part of what makes us live instead of simply exist. You and I simply have a great deal more than most. So..." He swallowed hard and watched the thoughts swirl through Faith's expressive eyes.

"Is this something you would be interested in? I mean, spending a very long life with me? Vampires live a long time unless something intervenes."

Faith's smile was nearly blinding. "I guess we'd better date for a while and find out. Although, I suspect this dating thing will have to happen regularly, for a very long time."

Aldric blinked.

Faith chuckled softly. "I mean that yes, I want to start this bonding process. Deliberately, I mean. With the intention of staying with you for a very long time. I..." Faith sighed.

She buried her head in his shoulder and breathed for a moment. And Aldric wrapped his arms around her, stroking his hand up and down her spine, trying to soothe whatever it was that upset her.

"The worst part about getting kidnapped was the thought that I'd never see you again. Then I had this thought, this *knowledge* that you were coming to save me and I was terrified that you were going to get killed. I couldn't stand that thought."

"I am well, Faith. I am here." Aldric soothed. "I have to admit, the thought that you were in the hands of those psychopaths made me insane. Marc had to talk me out of trying to save you on my own."

"I'm glad he did. Remind me to give him an extra hug in the morning," Faith said. She took a deep breath and leaned back to look him in the eye. "I love you, Aldric. I think I've been falling in love with you since you crashed in and killed a bunch of rogue werewolves in our kitchen, then turned around to treat me so carefully. I hope..." Her gaze faltered and she started staring at his shoulder. "I hope that you can maybe feel the same way someday."

"Faith." Aldric's heart had stopped racing at some point, and now he found himself calm and sure. "You are brave and fierce and loyal. You are determined and clever, and I have seen how kind you are to even complete strangers. You have saved my life several times, and you put up with my stubborn foolishness, and you singlehandedly saved the entire clan from further conflict this morning. I would be a stone-hearted fool not to love you already."

Faith grinned, joy shining from her whole self. Aldric could feel her magic brushing up against his skin, and he could feel himself responding to it.

"Well, Aldric Donnelly, Head Enforcer of the Frostwalker Clan. Maybe you should do something about it." Faith grinned. Her fingers danced over his shoulders.

"As you wish, Faith Latham, Magaestra of the Frostwalker Clan." Aldric bent and kissed her. He felt one of her hands leave his shoulder for a moment and then heard the door across the room close with a soft click of the latch.

And then there was nothing but the two of them and forever, which looked very appealing.

EXCERPT FROM CAROLINE'S INTERNSHIP

"Caroline! Welcome! We're all pretty excited to have you here." Point surged through a door on the other side of the short hallway like an elephant in a hurry.

Caroline blinked at him. He was just under six feet tall, but nearly as broad as the hallway, muscled, and had the typical slate grey skin and lumpy facial features trolls were known for. The button up shirt he wore was working hard to stay buttoned, and in the back of her mind Caroline was impressed that he could find suits that fit at all.

She'd been prepared to go down to Personnel to fill out paperwork today for her internship and start training. (Human Relations did, well, other things than dealing with employment paperwork and such.) It seemed, however, that Point had other plans.

"I'm glad to be here," Caroline answered. "I have to admit that I'm super nervous, though."

Point stopped them in the hallway, the sounds of a busy office flowing through the wide doorway just another foot further along their path, and turned to her.

"I would tell you that there's nothing to be nervous

about, but I'd be lying through my pointy teeth." He grinned, showing off the teeth in question. Caroline smiled back. Funny how Chief Point was absolutely not even a little scary to her, even with a mouth that a shark would envy.

"You really know how to reassure a girl," she said, and Point laughed.

"Yeah, well. I'm not going to bullshit you," he said. He dug in his pocket and pulled out an ID card on a lanyard. "There are probably going to be times where you're in a tight spot. I have every confidence you'll be fine, though, and I'm never sending you out there alone." His eyes twinkled for a moment and Caroline found herself somewhat disconcerted. "At least not until you graduate to full agent.

"Ah," Caroline said. She looped the lanyard around her neck. Point grinned again and patted her shoulder gently.

"Come on. Let's get you in there." He guided her that last foot and then around into the large room.

It looked almost like a stage set from a police procedural— desks pushed together in small islands, almost like a kindergarten classroom, worn office chairs and humming computers at each station, though she couldn't help but notice the number of clear, empty desks scattered around the room. It felt like a theatre during rehearsal— occupied and lively, but not quite where it should be in terms of occupancy.

The smell of coffee and something vaguely metallic hung in the air, and the ambient chatter in the room dropped significantly when they entered. Point sighed and stopped with what Caroline felt was a great deal of false reluctance.

"Folks, everyone listen up! For those of you that haven't met her yet, this is Caroline Peters, our new intern," he shouted. By the end of the sentence, the room was silent. "Many of you will remember her from the raid a few months ago. She'll be here for the next year at least, but if we're lucky she'll decide to stay with us for a while. Her hours are dependent on a number of things, not least of which being how badly you all behave. I will say this once, but I mean it. Behave or I will end you, if she doesn't do it first." Caroline blinked at him. She could tell that he was very serious about his threat, and she guessed that everyone else in the room knew it because there was a moment of surprised silence before someone started clapping. After a second the room was full of applause and friendly calls of 'welcome!' and 'who's throwing the good luck— I mean welcome— party?' and 'Anyone gives you any trouble, you can call me.' and 'I definitely remember how badass she was!'

Caroline picked out a few faces she recognized from the raid that had rescued her and Darien from the Elf Supremacists and all the aftermath from it. The tall, slim woman with streaks of green in her long black hair smiled and applauded. The blonde man sitting at a desk in the corner who waved and grinned at her while bouncing a red playground ball, and looked for all the world like he hoped they could play together at recess. There was the dark, sharp-looking man near what she thought might be the break room, since he was holding a coffee mug with steam rising from it, who grimly nodded his welcome and turned back into the room beyond.

She saw Ollie the ogre peek out and smile at her from another door, and blinked again. The ten foot tall ogre was wearing reading glasses and a lab coat and smiling broadly, and if she didn't see the puckered scar on his chin she would never have known it was the same mountain of rage that plowed straight through a wall to completely destroy a half dozen archers making a last stand from the kitchen during the raid.

Darien lounged in his desk chair and grinned so wide she was half afraid his head would fall off. She grinned back, feeling a bit less awkward. The bloodbond from back then had long since worn off, but they were still close. Darien had kept in touch after the kidnapping and raid, and they'd become pretty good friends. Even her parents liked him. Point steered her that way.

"Okay, okay, simmer down. You all have things to be doing, I'm sure. D, you take Caroline around, show her where everything is. I emailed you her training schedule this morning, so make sure she knows where she needs to be, and when." Point turned back to Caroline. "He'll take you down to personnel to get your paperwork finished up. I know you did most of it already, but there's always some damn thing. Your desk is here next to D, and I.T. should be by after lunch to get your computer set up. Till then, just get that paperwork done and make sure you know where everything is, or at least who to ask about whatever you're looking for."

"Okay. Got it." Caroline nodded and glanced at Darien who was still grinning.

"Hey there, Sunshine. You ready for the tour?" Darien asked.

Point made a face at him and simply muttered "Behave." As he walked towards what Caroline assumed was his office.

"Um, yeah," she answered.

"You don't have to look so spooked," Darien said, standing and stretching towards the ceiling. "Nobody here bites without express permission." He winked at her. Winked!

"Jackass," Caroline muttered, and he just laughed.

"Come on, We'll stop in the lab first. Ollie's been holed up in there for two days. You'll be a great excuse to peel him away from his microscope for a minute." Darien ambled off towards the door the ogre had poked his head out of a few minutes earlier, and Caroline had no choice but to follow.

The large laboratory was about what she expected, except that everything was made to accommodate the giant body of Ollie himself. Long tables, half of which were extra tall, with various pieces of equipment that she couldn't begin to identify positioned strategically. A rolling cart with various tools on the shiny metal top was pulled up next to a human-sized man while he held a light over a machine for a tiny woman with extremely long fingers who was prodding a tool inside.

"Caroline! I'm so happy you chose to take Point's offer!" Ollie's grin rivaled Darien's a few minutes ago. "I was extremely impressed with your ability to keep this idiot alive. You deserve a medal, in my opinion."

"Um, thanks?"

"Hey!" Darien objected loudly. "I was doing okay, thanks. Not that she wasn't badass or anything, but—"

"You were either bleeding out and dying, or you lied to the powers that be. Which is it?" Ollie smirked.

Darien grunted and frowned, and Ollie laughed.

"You'll keep this guy in line for us, won't you?" Ollie's eyes sparkled.

"I suppose. If it's really necessary." Caroline grinned back, feeling much less anxious than she had an hour ago. This was all going to be okay.

They left the lab a few minutes later, and Darien showed her the meeting rooms ,and the archive, and Human Resources where two very tired looking people sat on a sofa in the corner, drinking coffee and chatting.

"Hey D. What're you back this way for?" one of them asked. She was about Caroline's height, but her fingers were long and slim, like the woman in the lab, and her ears were even more pointed than an elf's.

"I'm showing Caroline around. It's her first day," Darien answered. "This is Caroline Peters, our new intern. Caroline, this is Stevie Goodleaf," the woman stood up and came over to shake hands. "And that is Nelson Wood" The elf on the sofa nodded and saluted with his coffee cup.

"Pleasure to meet you! We don't get a lot of actual humans around here. Mind if we pick your brain some?" Stevie asked.

Caroline gazed around the room with a sense of reverence. It was all lighted mirrors with chairs facing them, and several rolling cases of what looked like makeup tools. There was a shelf of wigs along one wall, and two rolling clothing racks that had zipped-up covers over them. There was a smell of powder and coffee and laundry soap in the air.

"You guys made Point look amazing when he came to the hospital! If I hadn't already seen what he really looks like I'd never have known he wasn't just a huge guy! You're amazing!" Caroline felt a little starstruck.

Nelson smiled and murmured "Thank you."

Stevie grinned. "Wow. You've got him gushing! I can tell that D's got more for you to do, but you come on by and have a coffee with us sometime. There's usually room on our couch when we're not neck-deep in an operation."

"Thanks, I will," Caroline smiled back and let Darien lead her away again. "Man, everyone's been really nice. I expected tough federal agents to be more… I don't know. Grumpy and overworked?"

Darien laughed and they turned to go up the stairs to the next floor. "We are that, too, a lot. But everyone's excited that you're here. I'm pretty tough, to be honest. I have faster reflexes than humans and elves, and I'm overall stronger, faster, and harder to hurt than a lot of other beings, and then I'm a trained agent. Those elves still knocked me out and damn near killed me. Then you, an untrained teenager came in and not only managed to get through the ordeal with just a few scrapes and bruises, but you saved my life, took down several of our captors on your own, and confronted an angry elven mage. That's not exactly unimpressive." They reached the top of the stairs and he turned to look her right in the eye.

Caroline blinked at him. "I... I guess I never really thought about it like that."

"Well, you should. We're all pretty excited to have such a badass human around here." He grinned at her again. "And I'm not going to lie. There's some folks who are jealous of me for getting to be your unofficial partner." A shadow flickered through his eyes and Caroline wondered if he minded having to start from the beginning with training her.

"Well, if you say so." Caroline shrugged, and followed Darien down towards the gym that took up half the floor.

ABOUT THE AUTHOR

Katherine Kim is a lifelong lover of fantasy. She started early, being read Tolkien as bedtime stories, which honestly explains a lot. More recently she's been drawn to more urban fantasy stories through both books and television, and reading continues to be a passion. She is an American that lives and writes in Tokyo, with her family.

If you liked this book, I hope that you'll leave me a review! I read every review and it makes a huge difference to me and to my work, but even just a few stars would make my day. Keep up with new releases, giveaways, and other antics by joining my mailing list. You'll get a free short story, news of my new releases and sales, and updates from any shenanigans I get up to!

BOOKS BY KATHERINE KIM

Spirits of Los Gatos

Sarah's Inheritance

A Spirit's Kindred

Finding Insight

Brewing Trouble

Spiritkind

Federal Paranormal Activities Agency

Quick Study (Prequel)

Caroline's Internship

Caroline's Christmas

In The Blood

Heavy Traffic

Vampire's Curse

Fighting Fire

Almost An Agent: Honor Among Thieves

No Honor Among Thieves

Properly Paranormal

The Magaestra Trilogy

Magaestra: Found

Magaestra: Loyalties

Magaestra: Tested

The Greenwoods Neighborhood: New to the Neighborhood

An Intellectual's Property

Away From Home